HOUSTON ISD
Cesar Chavez High School Library
8501 Howard
Houston, Texas 77017

WRITTEN IN FIRE

A Lobo Blacke/Quinn Booker Mystery

William L. DeAndrea

Walker and Company
New York

First published in the United States of America in 1995 by Walker
Publishing Company, Inc.

Published simultaneously in Canada by Thomas Allen & Son Canada,
Limited, Markham, Ontario

Library of Congress Cataloging-in-Publication Data
DeAndrea, William L.
Written in fire: a Lobo Blacke/Quinn Booker mystery/William L. DeAndrea.
      p. cm.
      ISBN 0-8027-3270-4
      I. Title.
      PS3554.E174W75   1995
      813′.54—dc20   95-11289
              CIP

Printed in the United States of America
2 4 6 8 10 9 7 5 3 1

1

I CLICKED OPEN the plain gold cover of my watch and checked the time. If train schedules could be relied upon (and my previous experience in the West had shown me that they might be relied upon just about as much as the kind of Wild West fiction I used to write), the Prairie Wizard should be arriving in Le Four in an hour or so.

I call it the Prairie Wizard because someone with access to a bucket of paint, a soul full of poetry, and not very much in the way of artistic talent had already done so, in the form of dripping white letters alongside the cab. It was, in fact, a very ordinary sort of train, not overly burdened with gleaming metal or glamour of any kind. However, its engine throbbed steadily, the wheels ate up the prairie below us, and the whistle was reassuringly throaty and shrill when it was called upon.

We were headed south, on a spur off the Northern line into the cattle country of the eastern Wyoming Territory. We'd passed over the unmarked line from Montana about thirty minutes before—again, depending on the reliability of the railroad's schedule makers.

Or, I must concede, upon the accuracy of my watch.

I am loath, however, to consider even the possibility of inaccuracy in that watch; it held virtues in my eyes far beyond its merits as a timepiece. It was at once a token of a friendship and the bribe that had caused me to embark on my present voyage. I did not know how long I would be in Le Four; I knew only that I held a one-way ticket.

I opened the watch again, this time to read the inscription.

Presented to Quinn Booker by Louis Bowman Blacke, his Partner in Words.

It was with difficulty that I suppressed a smile of satisfaction as I placed the watch back in my vest. I supposed I was the only man—and I was certain I was the only lowly *easterner*—to have been made a present of a gold watch by the legendary Lobo Blacke himself. In Blacke's previous career, when he made someone a present of metal, it was usually lead.

On the chance that you have somehow managed to avoid any exposure whatever to the lore of the western part of this continent, I will sketch the man's biography.

Born in Missouri about fifty years ago, the son of an antislavery preacher in that slaveholding state that could not bring itself to secede from the union, Blacke chose to fight for the North in the War between the States, which he did with distinction, being twice mentioned in dispatches from the front.

The end of the war left him, as it did so many of the other young men it touched, strangely torn. On the one hand, he was sickened by the waste and carnage of the war; on the other, he found that a taste of danger and a whiff of gun smoke held an awful exhilaration for him. He knew he would never be content to preach or farm or run a store for the rest of his days.

So, like so many others he turned to the West. He tried for a spell to be a cowboy; loved the riding and the trail and the countryside, but, as he told me when we were working on the book together, "Booker, I got almighty sick at looking at the ass end of a cow."

I of course rendered his language suitable for a family audience before publication. The language out here is the strangest mixture of poetry and profanity one can imagine. In fact, leaving aside questions of propriety, one must concede that a lot of it is the poetry *of* profanity.

But I digress. Blacke stopped following cattle and began following bad men as a U.S. marshal. He served at posts all through the West, and it soon came to be known that bandits who struck a town under the care of Lobo Blacke had best make two sets of arrangements beforehand—one set for the care of their families and belongings while they vanished for a long stay, and one set for their funerals.

Blacke was also the scourge of train robbers, so much so that he was once brought east to St. Paul, where he was taken to lunch by the great

James J. Hill, founder of the Great Northern Railway. Hill offered Blacke a job as chief of security, with a fat paycheck, a budget sufficient to pay a handpicked staff, and a fancy office in St. Paul, just down the hall from James J.'s own.

Blacke turned him down, a decision he says he has never regretted. For myself, I had my own (never expressed to Blacke) doubts about the matter. If he had been safely ensconced in an office in St. Paul, a city that passes for a metropolis out on the prairie just as the Catskills pass for mountains to a New Yorker such as myself, he wouldn't have taken the bullet that paralyzed him five years ago. In the unlikely event it had happened anyway, he would have had a staff of trained operatives on hand to investigate and avenge him.

I did not learn until much later that Blacke might have availed himself of the latter in any case. Shortly before I met him, when he was still bed-ridden in a hotel in Boulder, Wyoming (where he'd been shot), Hill had come out and paid him a visit, offering Blacke the same job all over again.

Blacke had again refused, and Hill went away scratching his own head and muttering that the bullet must have affected Blacke's brain as well as his spine.

As I was to learn later, that was in one sense true.

In any event, it was shortly thereafter that I made the acquaintance of the legendary Mr. Blacke.

I was making my first trip to the West. Like Blacke before me, I was seeking change and adventure, although I admit in a much milder way. The only rebellion I had part of was my own against my family. I was raised in New York—part of the time in the city with my maternal grandparents, whose blushes in society I shall save by not mentioning their names in what they would be sure to consider (along with the rest of my writings) as sensationalist trash. Summers and vacations I spent at West Point, where my widowed father, Colonel Bogardus "Bayonet Eyes" Booker, was an instructor.

My father had always assumed that I would follow him into the army, after a term at the academy, of course. He had already arranged an appointment for me.

I balked. I told him I did not desire to go into the army, especially since our beloved country was not at war and no war seemed immediately in prospect. Should the situation change, I told him, I would of course do my duty.

The discussions became rather heated. I remember at one point telling my father that since I had spent my entire life taking orders from a colonel, I considered any military obligation I might have had in theory to be paid in full.

I have regretted that statement since, but not much. The upshot was that while he has not actually gone so far as to disown me, relations between us have been strained since. My grandparents (who had never truly approved of their daughter's marrying a military man in the first instance) offered me their roof while I attended Columbia University. But come graduation, I found Granddad had planned a life for me more regimented than that of any soldier, right down to the office I was to occupy and the girl I was supposed to marry in furtherance of the empire of business.

That was enough to jolt me loose. My mother had left me a (small) independence, which I came into on my twenty-first birthday. I used it to take a room downtown near Printing House Square and proceeded to make my living with my pen.

And I prospered, both as a journalist and as an author of popular fiction. Granted, although the money I made from the *Herald* and from the western stories I cobbled together from scraps of spare time and imagination for what are popularly known as "dime novels," made me the merest fraction of what Granddad had been prepared to pay me, I lacked nothing in food, warmth, diversion, and companionship.

Soon, I was doing so well with the stories, I could leave the world of day-to-day journalism completely. I resolved, since the source of my independence was there, to travel to the West and accumulate some firsthand impressions with which to color my stories.

I was amazed. I learned that the real West was at once infinitely more mundane and infinitely more wonderful than I had imagined— indeed, more so than I *could* have imagined.

Mundane, because all the staples of my fiction—gunfights, Indian fights, and the rest—were rare. The gunfights, at least, were no more common than those in the most lawless areas of Manhattan. The very reason that incidents like the O.K. Corral became legendary was expressly because they did not happen all the time. Incidentally, if everyone who claims to have been a witness to that famous gunfight had actually been there, Tombstone, Arizona, would have been more populous than New York, Chicago, and Philadelphia combined.

Still, I found the West a land of wonders. It was not the land of timeless myth, peopled by Titans, as I had imagined, true. It was something better. It was a land where ordinary people had the space, the time, and the lack of constraint that too-long established government and conventional society bring to be themselves. In the West, men and women could grow into whatever odd shape Providence had intended for them, without getting the edges rubbed smooth and the odd corners knocked off by constant rubbing against their fellow citizens, or against the past.

I was at once elated and afraid. How could I reflect this new knowledge in my work? One would have to be a westerner, I thought, to adequately reflect this way of life, and though I might admire and love the West, might even be in it, my upbringing guaranteed I would never be of it.

Then, one day, I came to the town of Boulder in the Wyoming Territory, where Lobo Blacke was healing from the cowardly shot in the back that had paralyzed him from the waist down.

I wangled my way in to see him. I expected to find him morose and angry. Instead, I found him propped up on the bed, smoking a vile cigar and perusing a *Police Gazette* as a young, but shall we say experienced, lady shaved him with a straight razor.

He looked up from his magazine.

"Nice suit," he said. "Where'd you get it?"

I gave him the name of my tailor in New York.

"I like a good set of clothes. My niece, Becky, here, likes a man in good clothes, don't you, darlin'?"

Becky was wearing an emerald green robe over nothing much. Even at this hour of the morning, her eyes were outlined in kohl and her lips were crimson. She looked at me with an appraisal frank to the point of brazenness, but also with a smile that bespoke genuine good humor and regard for the man in the bed.

"He's not bad," she said. Then she laughed and added, "Uncle, dear. Move your cigar before I cut it off." She began shaving under his nose.

"So," he said through tightened lips. "What I can do for you, Mr. . . .?"

"Booker. Well, sir. I've already accomplished one of my aims; I've met you."

"Disappointed, are you?"

"No sir."

"No? Hell, I would be. Big lawman feared by all the scum of the West. Clancy the manager tells me you're a writer; ain't that how you writer fellas would put it?"

"Most likely," I admitted.

Blacke grunted. "Well, I'm not much of a scourge now. I'm a help-less cripple can't even keep his balance enough to sit on the privy by himself, and who has to be shaved by his, um, niece. Isn't that what you see?"

"I see a man who has done remarkable things bearing up well after an incident that would have crushed most men."

He reached up with a clumsy hand and took the cigar from his mouth. The short, thick bush of prematurely white hair on his head seemed to bristle. His eyes narrowed, and suddenly the word "scourge" seemed much less a foolishness of an eastern writer.

"Let me tell you two things, Booker. I am not bearing up well. On the inside, I'm screaming with hate, but Becky didn't shoot me, and neither did you. There's no sense in delivering a load to the wrong address."

"If you scream at me," Becky said placidly, "I'll cut your throat."

Blacke's face softened for a split second as he gave her a quick smile. Then he turned the narrow-eyed glare back to me.

"The other thing is, some son of a bitch deliberately shot me in the back. He planned to kill me; he failed. That was his mistake, because someday he's going to swing for it."

"You speak as if you know who he is."

"I don't," he said darkly, "but I will. I know what I was doing when I got this, and there's only a limited number of people who might have wanted to stop me."

He shook his head.

Becky hastily pulled the razor away. "You'll lose an ear that way, you fool." She blotted a thin line of blood with a towel, reached for a styptic pencil.

"All right, all right," he said. He didn't wince as she applied the collodion. "I just didn't want to give our eastern friend here the idea I'm not the bitter old crock he expected to find." He turned to me again with the deceptively open expression he'd worn at first.

"All right, Booker," he said. "What can I do for you?"

"What I have in mind is something we can do for each other, Mr. Blacke."

"All right, spit it out."

"I think I should help you write your memoirs."

Lobo Blacke was not a man used to being surprised, but this surprised him. "My memoirs? What's the point? People like you have already printed more lies about me back east than I could ever live up to."

I nodded. "People like me, yes, but, if it makes a difference, not me personally. I have had only fictitious heroes perform fictitious feats."

"And done right well at it, to judge from your outfit. I'm not about to lend my name to another pack of lies."

"No, sir," I said. "The truth, as much as possible in your own words."

"Why?" he asked.

"Because through you, I hope to get close to understanding the land and people out here. And, not to put too fine a point on it, I believe *The Memoirs of Lobo Blacke, Dictated by Himself*, as told to Quinn Booker, will sell many thousands of copies. It could make us both very comfortable men."

"I'm comfortable now," Blacke said.

I nodded. "And well cared for, too," I said. "However, I gather from Clancy that he is not charging you for your room and board, and the doctor is likewise treating you for free."

He looked at me for a moment in silence. "Clancy has a big mouth," he said at last.

"I don't believe for a moment," I said, "that you are working a hardship on anyone. Clancy, in fact, told me in so many words that he considers your stay here to be a partial payment of a debt of gratitude he owes you for the protection you have afforded this town, and especially for your foiling a swindler who once almost cheated him out of this very hotel."

He replaced the cigar and bit on it. "A *real* big mouth," he said.

"I also don't believe for a second," I said, "that you are the kind of man who can live for long comfortably on gratitude."

He raised one black eyebrow. The gray eye under it glittered. "I've got to get used to having two sticks of dead meat for legs. Maybe I can get used to living on gratitude, too. You never know what you can do if you have to."

"You don't have to, Blacke," I said impatiently. "That's the point. And what about your plan to find the one who did this to you? Even a lowly easterner can tell you you're not about to fork leather and ride off in pursuit. Your detective genius no doubt remains intact, but you will need to hire people with healthy legs to bring you facts to work on."

Becky wheeled on me with anger in her eyes hot enough to glow through the blackness around them. "Now you just look here—" she began.

I was glad I was out of razor reach.

Blacke put one of his clumsy hands on her arm. "Shh, darlin'," he said. "Always give a man credit for saying what he truly thinks. It saves time."

Still fuming, Becky scraped the last bit of lather off Blacke's chin and wiped his face with a towel. The ex-lawman felt the newly pink skin and said to me, "Thank you, Booker. That's a fact I've been trying to face for some time. Didn't want to, but if a tenderfoot like you can see it, it must be true. Do you really figure I can make some money on this deal?"

"Very strongly, but no guarantees."

"Let's give it a try, then."

I came to the bed, and with Becky eyeing us warily, shook hands on it. His hand was a bit shaky, but very strong.

I moved into the hotel. Every day, all day, for seven weeks, Lobo Blacke told the story of his life. In addition to his other virtues, he was a natural-born storyteller, with an eye for telling detail and a knack for arranging facts in their most effective order, a trait that must have stood him in good stead during his lawman days.

For those seven weeks, I got to live the life of a westerner, albeit vicariously. And by the time we were through, I knew I had something much more worth reading, and much more powerful, than the fairy tales I had constructed before.

I was reluctant to leave, but the next step had to be taken in New York. So confident was I in the success of our venture that I decided to arrange with Mr. Scribner to meet all the expenses of publication myself, and therefore reserve a greater share of profits to Blacke and me.

It was a wise move. The book's success exceeded my expectations, and suddenly I was in great demand in New York, both in writing and lecturing. Sending Blacke the checks for his half of the profits brought me almost as much pleasure as cashing my own. After I sent the first one, I received a telegram that read as follows:

```
YOURS  RECEIVED  WITH  THANKS.  EXTRA
REMUNERATION  RECEIVED—CLANCY  BET  YOUD
SWINDLE ME. REGARDS BLACKE.
```

After that, I had to send the checks with almost religious zeal, if only to give Clancy the lie about my character. Each time, I received telegraphic acknowledgment from Blacke. A year and a half ago, I received a change of address, to Le Four, Wyoming Territory. I consulted an atlas and found it to be a vigorous and growing town at a railhead in the northeastern part of the territory, on the plain west of the Black Hills of Dakota.

I'd wondered what had happened in Boulder and wrote a letter asking, but got no reply other than this:

```
A JOB IS YOURS IF YOU WANT IT. COME TO LE
FOUR SOONEST. I NEED YOU BOY. REGARDS BLACKE.
```

"I need you." The old master had done it gain. Even if I felt none of the admiration and regard for the man that I did, curiosity alone would have drawn me westward, just to see what the old lawman had in mind.

2

WHOEVER NAMED THE town "Le Four," which is French for "The Oven," must have done so in the summertime. Now, in late November, the sky was as gray as the dust of Main Street and the weathered wood of the buildings that lined it. The wind not only bit, it had claws as well. Even the dust particles it blew before it felt cold when they hit exposed flesh.

I hunkered down into my greatcoat and tucked it tight across my neck with my left hand while I reached for my valise with my right. I had already arranged for my trunk to be brought after me.

There was quite a crowd at the station, but they hadn't come to greet me. They were there to see the professor: to look at the pictures he'd taken of the wilderness and to have their own faces recorded for posterity.

The professor's name was Edward Belking Vessemer, but you've undoubtedly heard of him as Professor Ned and seen the engravings based on his photographs in *Frank Leslie's Illustrated Newspaper* or similar publications.

I was prepared to dislike the man when I met him. As a writer myself, I have always resented the ancient Chinaman's assertion that "one picture is worth ten thousand words," but Professor Ned came closer to making that true, at least of the West, than any other man I had ever heard of. I might have written (both before and after my actual experience of the West) of the glint in the eye of the gunman, the dignity and pride of the Indian chief, the stubbornness of the pioneer family, or the wild beauty of the landscapes of the West.

But Professor Ned captured them for you, trapped them with some arcane science on pieces of glass or paper, and preserved them for all to see.

Being among the only first-class passengers on the train, we met in the dining car with some frequency. Common politeness required we acknowledge each other, which we did with increasing cordiality, until we ended by sharing a few meals.

The other evening over a buffalo steak, I remarked that I was surprised that he did not take his meals in that famous Pullman car of his, the one he had persuaded the Great Northern to build for him when he took the post of official photographer to the railroad.

"Shouldn't be surprising at all," he said quietly. His voice was habitually quiet, to the point where the stranger might make the mistake of taking it for diffidence.

Diffident men, after all, do not comb the West challenging the white, red, black, and yellow races to produce their most savage faces for him to photograph; they do not tramp for days through uncharted wilderness in search of vistas previously unseen.

"My Pullman," he went on, "is at once my studio, laboratory, and living quarters. I will admit that there are cooking facilities in this last, but they were included before I realized that neither I nor Henry, my assistant, has the first idea of how to cook anything. If it weren't for the dining car, we'd starve. Henry is not even with me this trip—he is back in Minneapolis with a badly broken leg."

I smiled. He returned it, and reached into his pocket for a leather cigar case, removed something long and gray that lacked only the sheen of oil to be mistaken for a gun barrel, and offered me its twin.

I declined with thanks. I will indulge in the guilty pleasure of a chaw on rare occasions, but since living through the fire that killed my mother, I am constitutionally unable to deliberately draw hot smoke into my lungs.

Vessemer had no such reservations, and he sucked the flame toward the tip of his cigar with such obvious pleasure that I nearly envied him.

"These, Booker," he said to me, "are the things that make my career possible. I can't function without them."

"There is something I should like very much to understand," I said.

"What is that?"

"Why being photographed is such an unpleasant experience."

He drew himself up a little at that. "I flatter myself that my subjects don't find it so. Have you never been photographed?"

"As a child. I mainly remember the sittings as occasions for my father to get angry with me and tell me that if I didn't stop fidgeting, he'd give me five with the flat of his sword."

"Then the photographer was an incompetent fool."

"He was well thought of among the officers at the Point," I told him.

"No doubt. Some perverse compulsion to turn what should be a pleasant experience into an uncomfortable duty. It is the duty of the photographer to pose his subjects in the proper manner. I have written a monograph on the subject, for my fellow artists, but I can sum it up for you in three points. The photograph must be true to the subject. The pose must be comfortable for the subject. And the elements of the photograph must be composed as carefully as a painter composes the elements of his own design.

"In fact," he went on, "we must do it even more carefully."

"Why?" I asked.

"Because the painter has the whole range of color available to his use; we photographers have only shades of gray. Further, it takes time for the light to etch its image on the chemicals on the plate. During those moments when the shutter is open, all must be serene and comfortable for the sitter."

"Surely," I said, "it takes far longer for someone to paint a portrait."

"But it's not the same thing, Booker, don't you see? If someone were painting your portrait, it might take weeks, but the painter will, so to speak, blend all your fidgeting into an average position.

"A photographer can't do that. We arrange the elements, and God's own daylight does the actual painting. In actual fact, light itself is the subject of every photograph. If a sitter fidgets during the moment the light reflects from him into the lens, he will leave but a blur."

I was fascinated. I love learning the details of the everyday work of the world, perhaps because, aside from my writing, I have never actually done any. That is, not for money. In the course of indulging my interest, I have learned how to do many things, after a fashion.

But right now, I was questioning the professor. "Why is it, then," I asked, "that one almost never sees a smiling face in a photograph?"

He showed me a smile on his own face. It was a pleasant smile, for all that it was at this moment disfigured by the room it had to make for the cigar.

"It's a question I have wondered about myself," he admitted. "One reason is that while physiologists have shown that it actually takes less effort to sustain a smile than it does a frown, it still takes some effort, and a smile can slip at the last moment and turn a pleasant face into a smudge. A relaxed face, in almost all cases, looks somewhat stern."

He took a puff. His cigar glowed bright red.

"But there's more to it than that," he said. "It's not *that* difficult to sustain a smile."

"What is it, then?"

"A sense of history. Most of the photographs I've taken on my annual visits to Le Four have been of prosperous men and their families. This is for the generations to come, that they might marvel at the manner of people who wrested this particular fortune from the West. It is my opinion, Mr. Booker, that they wish to leave the impression that every moment of the task was serious, hard work. No frivolous descendant will get an excuse for idleness or pleasure from his ancestor's photo."

"And you go along because . . ."

"Indeed. I go along because my first principle is to be true to the subject, and a certain self-righteous priggishness is all too true to many of my subjects. This perhaps answers your next question."

"I beg your pardon."

"You were going to ask why I drag through the wilderness like a frontier scout, seeking new vistas and new visages, were you not, when I can make an embarrassing amount of money just taking my portraits?"

"The thought had occurred to me."

"It usually does to everyone, and I usually tell them it is to record the history of the West before civilization brings its inevitable changes, and there is an element of truth to that. But you bring out an urge to frankness in me, Mr. Booker, that surprises me. The real reason is that I am seeking subjects who have nothing to prove; who will let me capture their essence for the sake of my art, rather than for their self-aggrandizement."

"Perhaps more photography is the answer," I suggested.

"What do you mean?"

"I mean that most people are photographed only once or twice in their lifetime. An occasion that rare is an invitation to somberness. If somehow photography were to become commonplace—or at least more common—people might be willing to expose more of their everyday good nature."

He grinned at me under his moustache. "So you think people have everyday good natures, do you?"

"Not all of them," I conceded, returning the grin. "But enough to make the statement true."

"You may meet nicer people than I do," he said. "But your point is well taken. Who knows? Photography has already progressed from needing hours to complete a picture to needing a minute or so. Perhaps science can make it easy enough for everyone to do so. I would be out of a job."

I shook my head. "You are more than a taker of pictures. You are an artist. The world has need of artists, and always will."

"Thank you, Mr. Booker," he said. He wished me good evening and returned to his private car.

I had hoped to speak to him when the train arrived. It occurred to me that it might be good for future editions of Blacke's autobiography to have a photograph tipped in as a frontispiece. Even injured as he was, the grizzled ex-lawman was formidable looking, probably as the result of his being actually formidable. A photograph of the man might help boost sales even higher. Some of the more fanatical of Lobo Blacke's devotees (and he had them—I forwarded the letters), who had already bought some previous edition, might purchase another in order to obtain the picture.

The hard part, I was sure, was to get Blacke to agree to it. "The biggest mistake I ever made," he once told me irritably, "was ever to let anybody get away with calling me 'Lobo.' If I'd stayed plain Louis Blacke, I'd still have two good legs."

It was an interesting theory, if unprovable. He believed it, though, and it had given him an unhealthy distaste for profit-maximizing publicity.

I was walking along the wooden platform in front of the station, working on ways I might induce Blacke to go along, when I heard a woman's voice calling my name.

"Mr. Booker?" it said again.

"Yes," I said. "I'm Quinn Booker."

I looked at the owner of the voice. Even in the cold, dust-laden wind that stung my eyes as I stood there, she was worth looking at. Of medium height and full and graceful form, she had a lovely, shining mass of tawny curls on her head under a fur-trimmed hat. She had a matching cloak and muff, and was as stylishly turned out as any Society girl might be on Fifth Avenue. She had long dark lashes over deep blue eyes, and a mouth at once demure and generous.

I tipped my hat and told her I was at her service.

She laughed at that, very musical, and said that she'd been sent to do a service for me.

"I'm to show you the way to the newspaper office," she said. "Mr. Blacke wanted to come to meet you in person, but Dr. Mayhew forbade it. The cold does make his legs ache, you know."

Suddenly, she offered an elegant hand, clad in a long, pearl gray glove. When I took it, her grip was surprisingly strong for a woman's.

"But I'm forgetting my manners," she said. "I'm Rebecca Payson. It's a pleasure to meet you again."

"Again?" I said stupidly. I looked once more at her face. It was infinitely prettier without the rouge and kohl.

"Becky?" I said.

"If you like. Mr. Blacke calls me that. I doubt that this wind will get any warmer; let's talk while we walk, all right?"

"A very wise suggestion," I said.

I offered her my arm; she took it. When she spoke again, her voice was very low, almost too low to be heard under the thin whine of the wind.

"I'm glad to be the one to meet you, Mr. Booker. I want to explain something to you."

"There's nothing you need to explain to me."

"There is. You knew me . . . before. You know what I was."

"A devoted friend to Louis Bowman Blacke. Aren't you still?"

She looked up at me. Her eyes seemed to have captured all the honest blue that had been drained from the overcast sky.

"More than ever," she said. "I'm his housekeeper and his nurse and his confidante, when he confides in anyone. But everything else is gone from my old life, do you see? Well, except for the fact that I still pretend to be his niece."

"You mean you're *not*?" I gasped.

"Please don't mock me, Mr. Booker. I have a new life here. I have respectability I'd despaired of. Do you know that *Reverend Mortensen* tips his hat to me?"

"Reverend Mortensen is a gentleman," I said, "and you are, and to me have always been, a lady."

"I asked you not to make fun of me."

"I'm not," I assured her. "I was raised among a lot of people to whom appearances were everything."

"Everybody's like that," she said.

"Not everybody. Blacke's not like that. I'm not. Appearances are external—if you're lucky, you get enough experience to judge a person by what's inside."

"I'm not so wonderful," she said, "inside."

"I think you kept Blacke alive. I think—well, never mind what I think. Let's just leave it that when I knew you before I conceived an admiration and respect for you that continues today. If your new mode of life adds to your happiness, I would die before I did anything to ruin it."

"Thank you," she said.

"For what?" I said. We walked on.

3

O N   A   M A P , Le Four looks like an uppercase letter *T* lying on its side with the crossbar to the east. The train station takes up most of the street (called, appropriately enough, Railroad Street), and Main Street runs off it due west.

We passed a couple of hotels, but Rebecca would have none of it. A room had been prepared for me in the *Witness* building, and I would live there.

We walked the wooden sidewalk, she telling me of the major stories the newspaper had recently run, I telling her as best I could about what the latest fashions in New York looked like. People smiled and said hello as we passed, and I did see a stern-looking man in clerical garb doff his round hat to her.

It was all rather pleasant if you could ignore the cold and the wind and the dust.

It was pleasant, that is, until we passed one of Le Four's multitudinous saloons. A group of young louts was hanging around outside. They had the unmistakable look of men who have drunk up their last dollar and now can't bring themselves to leave the place where they had spent it.

I didn't know what they did. They probably called themselves cowboys, but the true cowboys I had known were not idlers. They worked as hard at gambling and drinking as they did at punching cattle, and when the money was gone, they instantly went back to try to earn some more.

These young men, none of them as old as myself, I'm sure, were just looking for trouble.

"Whoo!" one of them exclaimed. "Looks like they just stepped off a weddin' cake."

"Yeah, Frank, well cut me a piece."

There were two more. All laughed.

"We can all have a slice," Frank said. "I'm in the mood for something sweet."

"That's enough," I said quietly.

The leader, Frank, a little bigger and perhaps a glimmer more intelligent than the rest, said, "Enough of what?"

"Enough of your filthy mouth," I told him.

"Hey, he had a bath last week," one of his companions said.

"Filthy Frank," said another, and they all laughed.

Frank didn't like that.

"We'll say what we like," he sneered at me.

I made a concession. "Speaking for myself, gentlemen, I have a thick skin, so say what you like about me. I'll take it in the jesting spirit in which I'm sure it's intended."

I took a step closer and widened my grin.

"However, Frank—may I call you Frank?—I'm not prepared to practice the same tolerance in the presence of a lady."

"Lady?" said a skinny youth with tousled black hair and a patchy beard. "You see a lady, Frank?"

"Shut up, Curly," Frank said. Turning his attention to me, he added, "Do you know who we are?"

I was still smiling. People have told me I do that when I'm getting angry; I myself have never observed it, of course, but if it's true it might explain the shocked reaction that usually follows when I do lose my temper.

"Well, I know that you're Frank, and this young man is Curly," I offered. "I've yet to be introduced to the other two."

"This is Bud," Frank said, introducing a burly giant who wore a tiny Stetson on a shaven head, "and this is Marvin." A youth who might have been Frank's younger brother (and, I found out later, was) stepped forward. He doffed his hat and made a sweeping, mocking bow in the direction of Rebecca.

I could feel the skin on my face get tighter.

"Pleasure," I said. "I'm—"

"I know who you are. We know all about you. You're that eastern dude who's coming to write for Blacke's newspaper."

"Quinn Booker," I said.

"All the same to us. You just write this for the old cripple. We work for Lucius Jenkins. Without Lucius Jenkins, you don't have a town here. So we do what we want, and we say what we want."

I had a sudden thought.

"Rebecca," I said. "Are they serious?"

"What do you mean?"

"Did Blacke arrange this as a hazing for me or something?"

"Did he . . . ? No. Let's just move on, Mr. Booker. These men are well known in Le Four."

"You mean, they're not a show put on for my benefit?"

"What are you talking about?"

"A bunch of ill-mannered louts hazing the 'eastern dude' right off the train—it's just like what I used to write in my dime novels. Any second now, they'll be threatening to make me 'dance.' "

Bud spoke for the first time. His voice began and died in a deep-throated mumble, but in between, it was possible to make out the words "not a bad idea."

It was time to bring matters to a head.

"As long as I am in this town, you will neither do nor say what you want in relation to the lady—or any lady, for that matter—and me. And you will apologize to her, right now."

A small crowd had gathered by this point; that suited me fine.

"And what if I don't?" Frank demanded.

"Frank," I said, "you are a boor and a fool, but you are something even worse than that—you are trite."

He narrowed his eyes at me. I think I was supposed to tremble.

"To answer your question," I went on, "I will have to make you."

He goggled. "Are you threatening to draw down on *me*?"

"I'm not armed," I said.

Rebecca was now pulling my sleeve. "Mr. Booker—Quinn—please, let's get out of here."

"In a few moments, dear," I told her.

Frank was angry at me now for not playing the game.

"Not armed? Well, you're just a goddam lunatic, Booker, because *I am*."

He brandished a large Colt .45, chrome plated, in front of my face. It was a beautiful weapon, and it gleamed in the feeble winter sunlight.

My eyes and nose combined to tell me that Frank spent much more time cleaning his pistol than he did cleaning himself.

"Those are made in Connecticut, you know," I said conversationally.

"*I don't care where they're made!*" he shouted. He wasn't quite jumping up and down in fury, but he was close. His companions drew back into the doorway of the saloon, as though to give Frank room to make his play, whatever that might be.

Frank pointed the gun at me. "No matter where it comes from, it can send you straight to hell!"

"You, too," I said. "What you're talking about is the preannounced murder of an unarmed man in front of a number of witnesses. A large number," I said, turning around to look at the still-gathering crowd. "You'll hang for that. You'd hang even if you worked for God Almighty."

I won't deny that I felt relief when Frank took the gun out of my face, but I tried hard not to show it, since my plan was to betray no fear in any case.

"Now," I said, "why don't you give the gun to Curly, and then try to strangle me or something? We'll get this settled quickly then, and you won't be liable for prosecution."

"I think I'll do just that," he said.

Keeping his eyes on mine, he held his gun up, butt first. Curly took it, and Frank came at me.

He was such a fool, it was a wonder, living as he did in a land where most men went about armed, that he had survived as long as he had.

He actually lunged for my throat, as though I'd suggest that to him without being ready for it. He was so obvious, I didn't even bother to duck, just gave him three hard punches, right, left, right, to the soft part of the belly. The next left hit him on the chin, not because I had any desire to bruise my knuckles, but because Frank's legs had turned to taffy, and he sank into it.

I stepped back and let him fall.

At that, he was tough. He never did go all the way down. When he hit his knees, he took away one of the hands that had been clutching his stomach and braced himself on the ground. He stayed there while he proceeded to vomit.

His retching was the only sound—his cronies and the crowd shocked into silence, I suppose. I felt a sense of real accomplishment.

Frank retched again. I said, "The lady will take that for an apology."

Rebecca took a tight hold of my arm. It felt very nice. I removed my left glove with my teeth, and examined my knuckles and flexed them. No serious damage done.

I looked around at the crowd, said good day, and tipped my hat. At the edge of the crowd, I saw what appeared to be a monstrous eye with smoke coming up from it. A camera. Professor Ned's moustached face appeared from behind it and winked at me. I waved back at him.

"Shall we go?" I asked Rebecca. "Blacke must be worried about us by now."

"By all means," she said. "I thought he would kill you. I mean—I had no idea you could . . . ?"

"My dear, a man who has spent nearly all his life on army bases, a man who has been raised by someone whose career has been spent training soldiers to fight, can't help but—"

"Booker, behind you!" It was the professor's voice. I turned just in time to get a glimpse of Marvin, Frank's brother, running at me. His eyes were wild.

I let the lunge come, ducked, grabbed Marvin by his gunbelt, and threw him over my back. He landed heavily on his own back. I had my knee on his chest before he could get his breath back.

I grabbed a handful of the scraggly beard and pulled the chin back. I raised my right fist over the exposed throat.

"Do you want to feel it smash?" I asked him. "Stop struggling or you will."

He stopped.

"Listen," I said. "You are going to keep still now, and the professor is going to take a picture of us, just like this."

"Glad to," the professor said. He began fussing with his apparatus.

"As soon as he's done," I went on, "I am going to the office of the Black Hills *Witness*, and I am writing an account of how an eastern dude had a cowardly employee of Lucius Jenkins begging for mercy. Do you know why I'm going to do that?"

Marvin lay still beneath me, breathing heavily with his eyes wide.

"Answer me!"

"No." It came out a squeak.

"Because, whereas Frank is merely a bully and fool, you, my boy, are a coward. And I do not like cowards."

"He had a knife, you know," came a voice from the crowd.

"I like murderous cowards even less. How are we doing, Professor?"

"Nearly done. Don't move."

We held our pose for what seemed an eternity, but what really must have been about twenty seconds. Then the professor said "All done," and I got up off Marvin and watched him walk away.

He started yelling at the professor. "You'd better not print that picture, if you know what's good for you," he warned.

"Marvin!" I snapped, and the youth jumped.

He turned on me. His eyes were hot with hatred.

"Keep your dirty little mouth shut and go back to your friends."

He pointed a finger at me. "You . . . you'd better start carrying a gun."

"I'll let you know if I do."

I took Rebecca's arm once more, and we completed our walk.

4

LOBO BLACKE WAS sitting in the composing room with his wheel-chair pulled up to a small table when we arrived. Seated across from him was a lean, pink-shaven gentleman about Blacke's age. The man was bald with a gray fringe, and he had small eyes of the deepest black. It was a shiny, hard black, like obsidian, not a warm black, like coal. His head gleamed in the light.

Between the two of them was a battered checkerboard, and they stared at it as intently as any generals I had ever seen could stare at the map of a battlefield.

I don't think they even noticed we were there until Rebecca could hold it in no longer.

"Uncle Louis, we had some trouble on the way here from the station. Frank and Curly and Bud and Marvin tried to pick on Mr. Booker—"

Blacke held up his hand. "Shh, Becky. Just a second, while I pin this old buzzard's ears back."

The black eyes looked up. His voice was a rasp, toward the tenor end of the register rather than the baritone.

"You'll do nothing of the—"

He stopped because Blacke was moving his piece. He jumped three of his opponent's men and laughed as the bald-headed man sat there sputtering.

"Do you concede?" Blacke demanded.

The bald man waved a hand.

"Okay, that's three games apiece for today," Blacke said. "I had mercy on you."

Finally, the ex-lawman looked at me. This was all to the good. I had been on the verge of being offended. The look reassured me, as did the broad wink that went with it.

"Booker!" he said, wheeling his chair around and offering me his hand. He was fleshier than he had been the last time I'd seen him, not far from corpulent, but his grip had the iron of old. "I'm glad to see you made it here all right."

"An excellent trip," I said. "The most dangerous part of the whole business was the walk from the train station."

"What happened?"

At that, Rebecca burst in and gave a somewhat overblown account of what was really a rather simple instance of teaching some bullies not to judge by appearances.

So, after a period of listening to things like, "and then Frank was *sick* all over his chaps," and "and he made Marvin stay still while the professor took their picture. It was wonderful," I cut in.

"They simply needed a lesson in manners," I said. "I was in a position to administer one."

Blacke looked at me shrewdly. "I guess you did. Didn't he, Lucius?"

The bald man growled. Blacke went on, "Booker, I want you to meet Lucius Jenkins. Lucius owns the biggest house, the biggest ranch, the hotel, the general store, the bank, the wagonwright's, two saloons, the sheriff, and practically everything else in town, except the *Witness*. Oh. And when it comes to playing checkers, I own *him*."

"Pleasure," I said, and stuck out my hand. He had a sour look on his face, but he took it, for a brief moment at least.

"Booker," he said.

"If those animals I dealt with on the way over here are among your possessions as they claim to be, you might consider keeping them on a tighter leash. Not that I didn't welcome the exercise, mind you, but they were quite rude to the lady, and I won't have that."

I had to give him credit for this much—he got the hint.

He took a black bowler hat from the rack near the door (in a black suit with a gold-checked vest and a red tie, he was dressed more like a dude than I was) and held it awkwardly before him, like a boy at a social, asking a girl to dance for the first time.

"My men were out of line," he said at last. "I apologize. I'll see it don't happen again."

"Thank you, Mr. Jenkins," Rebecca said.

"Yeah. Well, I'll be going now, Blacke. Next week at the usual time?"

"Fine," Blacke said.

Jenkins clapped the bowler on top of his head and walked out.

Blacke watched him leave and kept looking at the door for a few moments after it closed. Then he roused himself and began putting the checkers away.

"Becky, darlin'," he said, "I want to talk business with Mr. Booker, here."

"All right," she said. "I'll see if Mrs. Sundberg needs any help in the kitchen."

"Now, you don't have to do *that*. You know how touchy she is about her kitchen. Go read a book or write a letter or something."

"Whatever you say, Uncle Louis." There was a little bit of the smile that reminded me of the woman I'd first seen shaving him down in Boulder. It somehow made me feel good to know that she hadn't erased *all* traces of her former self in the name of respectability.

I sat across the small table from him at his beckoning and waited while he took a pot off the nearby Franklin stove and two stout cups off hooks and poured two cups of coffee.

The coffee was hot and thick, and it took the rest of the residual chill from my bones as I sipped it. Blacke, whose throat was apparently lined with asbestos, drank his in long swallows.

He put the cup down.

"Booker," he said. "Booker, Booker, Booker. What am I going to do with you?"

I laughed. "You're the one who dragged me out here," I pointed out. "Didn't you know why?"

"Hell, *I* knew why; I just didn't expect you to ruin it within twenty minutes of the time you got to town, that's all."

"What did I ruin?"

His eyes rolled under the bushy gray eyebrows. "What did he ruin, he asks me. Just everything. Just my whole plan. You were supposed to be my secret weapon. Now you're about as secret as a boil on my nose."

"Secret weapon? In which war? I thought you wanted me out here to write for your newspaper."

"Well, that, of course. I've been writing the damned thing myself, with Becky's help. I'd thought after doing that book with you that this writing thing was a breeze, but it's damned hard work, and it will be a pleasure to have a professional around here to take up some of the load."

"Well, then."

"But that was only the *open* part of it. That was the excuse to get you out here."

"Here I am. That much of your plan worked."

"Thanks for nothing." He tightened his lips, scratched his chin, and made various others of the gestures a man makes when he is thinking about something he'd just as soon have go away.

I let him have his peace while I looked around the *Witness* press-room. It was a good, big room, not only pressroom but newsroom and composing room as well. Behind me was the door through which Jenkins had exited. Through there was a small anteroom with a desk for sales and the acceptance of advertising copy and the like. This, I learned later, was Rebecca's usual post. Over Blacke's shoulder, I could see the press, a good one, steam powered and reciprocating. There were machines for folding and bundling, as well. Along the wall to my right, there were drawers of California job cases and stones for typesetting. The empty floor in the middle was taken up with writing desks and a drawing table. It turned out that there was a young man in town who was quite clever with a drawing pen and a fair hand at engraving, and that he sometimes could be prevailed upon to prepare a plate for the paper.

The *Witness* published on Wednesdays and Saturdays. With this being Thursday, the place was quiet. Tomorrow, the bustle would begin again in earnest, with reporters (meaning me, I supposed) scribbling furiously, and the typesetters (I knew not who) filling composing sticks as their hands flew back and forth from the job case carrying the little lumps of type metal that resolved themselves into information and entertainment on the printed page.

It was an atmosphere I loved, and if no other part of Blacke's mysterious plan worked out, at least I would be able to take part in some of the work of putting out a newspaper. Even the anticipation of it was bracing.

The back of the ground floor was used for a kitchen, from which welcome smells were coming, and Blacke's living quarters.

Right now, he was still struggling with his decision.

It was the first time I'd ever seen him doing this, but he'd discussed the practice at length when we were preparing his autobiography. He had developed the technique of talking a problem (either to himself or to a patient listener) up to a certain point, then pursuing it in his head through the ramifications of different decisions he might make. Then he picked the one that "sounded" best to him and followed that course.

I was glad I knew about the practice. It might have made him seem indecisive otherwise.

At last he sighed, said "Right" to himself, and looked at me.

"Booker," he said, "in the time you knew me before, did I ever strike you as hankering to go into journalism?"

"No," I admitted. "It was a bit of a shock when I learned you'd started up the *Witness*."

"So why do you think I did it?"

"Well, I never could see you as a farmer."

"Especially not with two bum legs."

"And you've always been a person with something to do, something to chase. You've always been involved. With a newspaper, you can at least be chasing stories, even if you can't be chasing bandits. And no one is more involved in the community than a newspaperman. Births, deaths, marriages, business openings, bankruptcies, socials—they all come through you here at the paper."

"You're clever, Booker. Of course, I knew that. But I'm still impressed. Because you're close to the truth. As far as the second part, the thing about me being the clearinghouse for information for the whole town, that's right on the money. I've come to like that a lot, and that's why I'll keep the paper going after I do what I started out to do. But it wasn't the main reason."

"Then I have no idea."

"Like I said, you were real close with the chasing thing. Listen. What did you think of Jenkins?"

"I think he has miserable taste in his employees."

Blacke gave a short honk of a laugh. "Hell, that much is obvious. I meant, what did you think of the man himself?"

"Struck me the way a lot of prosperous men in the West strike me. Sure of himself in a business deal or in a checker game—"

"Even if he's hopeless at checkers, which he is. I have to work hard to lose half the games to him."

"Why on earth would you want to do that?"

"So he'll keep coming back. More coffee?" Without waiting for a reply, Blacke refilled our cups. "But I interrupted you. He's confident. What else?"

"Well, he's got that odd reaction to dudes like me; as if I'm looking down on him in some way, and he's afraid to resent it, God knows why."

"I can tell you that," Blacke said. "He's got a wife. Married her out of a saloon down in Denver some thirty years ago. She's a shrewd one—has suspicions of Becky, I'll wager—but now she's the Fine Lady. Wait till you see the house she made Lucius build; wait until you hear her talk about So-ciety and how primitive things are out here.

"You being an easterner, she's going to just love you, Booker, and her daughter even more so."

"Daughter?" I said, but Blacke went on.

"That's why Lucius thinks you look down on him. Because his wife has made his life a hell for thirty years for not having eastern styles and graces."

"You must have been friends with him a long time."

Blacke sat up straight—being paralyzed, he had to press his big hands down against the table to achieve it—and took a great big breath through his nose. He held it for about five seconds, then let it go.

"Yeah, we've been friends for a long time. We'll keep being friends right up to the minute I see him hanged."

5

"THERE IT IS," said Ole Sundberg, perhaps the most superfluous statement ever uttered in the Wyoming Territory.

Sundberg was a half-breed, son of a Swedish farmer and an Indian mother. He was a swift, a typesetter so skillful that he could get a job at top money at any paper in New York. When I told him so, he'd simply said, "Why?"

I had to admit he had a point. He had his wife (who cooked and cleaned for Blacke) and a job he was good at for a boss he liked.

He was even willing, on occasion, to drive a tenderfoot in a buggy some ten miles out of town to a social thrown by the would-be sophisticated wife of Mr. Lucius Jenkins.

The "it" in question was the Jenkins residence. It was a four-story Victorian that, had it been made of stone rather than of wood (lumber itself was hideously expensive on the plains; stone apparently was too much even for the resources of the wealthy Mr. Jenkins), would not have looked out of place on Fifth Avenue. To see the turrets and gingerbread scrollwork of the exterior, to see the lamps gaily lighting each window, was to want to rub one's eyes in the conviction that one was the victim of a hallucination.

The name of the place was Bellevue, though all there was to see from it was endless miles of gray scrub. I understood Bellevue to actually be located somewhere on the vast confines of Jenkins's ranch, but the day-to-day work and habits of the American cowboy were nowhere in sight.

It was late afternoon, and the winter dark was gathering fast, along with a quickening of the everlasting cold, dry wind. Sundberg pulled the buggy up to the porch to let me off.

"For God's sake, go home," I told him. "You'll freeze out here. I'll borrow a horse, or catch a ride from someone else."

"Don't worry, Mr. Booker. The steward here is Mrs. Sundberg's brother. I go around to the kitchen, they take care of me fine."

"Good," I said. "If I let you get frostbitten fingers, Blacke will never forgive me."

"I take good care, Mr. Booker."

Assured of that, I began to climb the stairs. As I did, I heard a voice call my name.

I turned but could see only a shadowy shape in the twilight.

"Who's there?" I asked the darkness.

"Me. Marvin Hastings."

He took a step nearer the house, and the illumination from inside made him visible. He had shaved, and now he looked a lot younger.

"What do you want?" I demanded.

"I want to talk to you."

"How this time? With a knife or a gun?"

"Just talkin'. Man to man."

"I'll give you the benefit of the doubt," I said. Either the witticism was lost on him, or he was so intent on getting his message across that he showed no reaction.

"The paper came out today."

"It comes out every Saturday." As I said it, I remembered the wild exhilaration of Friday night, all of Blacke's staff working like demons to get the *Witness* together.

"I read it. There wasn't nothing about me in it."

"No," I said. "We decided that to be news it had to be something that happened to someone the reader could imaginably care about."

"You're making fun of me," he hazarded.

"You ran at me with a knife, Marvin. You would have killed me."

"Sometimes, I lose my head."

"One day, they'll stretch your neck."

"No. Not me. I won't let that happen. But look, I just wanted to thank you for that."

I was astonished. I would not have judged Marvin Hastings to be the kind of young man to have that kind of a thank-you in him.

Or an apology either, come to that, but the next thing he said was, "I'm sorry I jumped you like that. I'm glad you kept me from hurting you or . . . Miss Rebecca."

"Apologies wouldn't have been much good if you'd succeeded," I said.

"I know that. It's just that when I'm with the other guys, they expect me to act . . . well, you know."

I did know. They expected him to act stupidly, and he had obliged them. I believe it's the same among all groups of young men. It would certainly explain a lot of the behavior I witnessed among the young officers and gentlemen at the Point.

"I accept your apology," I said. "Of course, what happened Thursday should never happen again."

"I won't bother you no more, mister, I promise."

"Not just me," I told him. "Anybody who comes to town. And not just you, either. I'm counting on you to wise up that whole little gang."

He swallowed, probably at the notion of reining in his big brother. "Um, okay. I'll do what I can."

"Fine," I said, and started up the stairs again.

But Marvin wasn't done with me yet.

"Uh, Mr. Booker?"

"Yes?"

"I got a favor to ask you."

I waited, but Marvin seemed content to stay silent all night. I was getting cold, so I said, "Out with it, for heaven's sake."

"Uh, you remember that picture you had Professor Ned take?"

"I remember it. I haven't seen it yet."

"Would you please—*please* not show it to Miss Abigail?"

I raised an eyebrow. Abigail Jenkins was the daughter of Lucius Jenkins and the belle of these parts. Blacke had told me to watch myself, or she'd eat me for breakfast, he didn't care what I'd learned about women back east.

"Why Miss Abigail in particular?" I asked.

"Have you met her yet?"

"That pleasure still awaits me."

"You'll know when you meet her. I think the world of Miss Abigail, and she always has a kind word for me. I'm ashamed of what I tried to do, and I'd just as soon not have her see the proof of what happened."

I shook my head at human folly. Not his, mine. A couple of days ago, this boy had tried to kill me; tonight I was feeling sorry for him.

"All right," I conceded. "I'll show Miss Abigail no pictures. And I won't mention it to her, either."

He smiled. Without the petulant look, he wasn't a bad-looking boy.

"Thanks, Mr. Booker. You're a good man."

"For an easterner."

"Yeah!" he said. "I mean, no. I mean, for anybody."

The smile melted from his face. "There's just one more thing. Can you fix this with the professor, too?"

"Why don't you ask him yourself? It's the manly way, and you're doing all right with it so far."

"I did ask him myself. He just laughed at me."

"I'll see what I can do," I told him.

He started to thank me again. If I let him do much more of it, I'd be snapping icicles off my ears, so I cut him short and went up to the door and knocked.

If the outside of Bellevue was the promise of Park Avenue on the prairie, the inside was the promise kept. Deep red carpeting. Flocked wallpaper from Paris. Cut glass from Holland. It might have been a magic door I'd walked through, sending me back to the world of my grandparents.

There were only two things to mar the illusion that I had walked through some sort of magic doorway that had annihilated the distance between the Black Hills and New York.

The first was that the lights were oil lamps instead of gas ones; the second was that the butler greeting me at the door was an Indian instead of an Englishman or a colored man. His livery was impeccable, as was his demeanor. Here was someone else who could write his ticket back east. A skillful butler who happened to be a red Indian would be the talk of Society.

He took my coat, opened the door to the ballroom, and announced me.

Instantly, a tall, handsome woman swooped down on me from across the room.

"Oh, Mr. Booker," she gushed. "Thank you so much for coming to my little soiree."

"I'm honored, madam. I presume you are—"

"Oh, where *are* my manners. Yes, I am Martha Jenkins." She held out her hand horizontally, expecting it to be kissed.

Well, far be it from me to disappoint her. I bent and kissed her hand, though it was no easy thing. The hand was soft enough, if a trifle large, but I nearly put my eyes out on some of the jewelry that projected from her fingers. It led me to wonder if Lucius Jenkins numbered a diamond mine among his assets.

If he didn't, then I was more impressed than ever with his wealth. Many a man has lived and died and worked hard the whole time in between and never come close to earning enough to purchase the jewelry on that one hand alone. Whatever it was Martha Jenkins "rode" her husband about, it wasn't about stinginess.

"And dear Mr. Booker, it is I who am honored to have you here. It's like a breath of fresh air to have someone visit who has something about him of the grace of the wider world."

"Odd," I said. "It would seem that fresh air was one thing available here in abundance."

She tilted her head back, veiled her mouth with jeweled fingers, and let a small titter escape her.

While she had her eyes closed in mirth, I took the opportunity to study her. She was a handsome woman, indeed. Tall, with a robust figure, large eyes, a strong nose, and a generous mouth, she had been intended, I was sure, for healthier pursuits than the aping of idle people some two thousand miles distant.

You might have taken her for thirty until you noticed the suspiciously red and uniform chestnut of her hair and the carefully powdered-in wrinkles at the corners of her eyes.

"And wit!" she said. "You won't believe what coarseness passes for humor around here."

"With you for a muse, madam, I shall be at my wittiest."

Even as I heard myself, I sickened myself. Fifth Avenue courtier was a role I could play, but it had nothing to do with my actual self. The necessity of playing that role was one of the things that had led me to flee New York.

Now I was slipping back into it without a moment's hesitation because it might be possible to salvage Blacke's original plan, the one that had led him to ask me to Le Four in the first place.

Because Blacke had taken his book-spawned wealth, moved to Le Four, and started the newspaper for one reason—to have an excuse to poke around his old friend Lucius Jenkins.

"His fortune is built on dirty money, boy," the ex-lawman had told me in the pressroom the other day.

Lucius had been a marshal with Blacke in the early days of Blacke's career.

"He was a good man to ride with, Booker. A thinker and a planner. Some of it rubbed off on me, but in those first days, I would have ridden into a new ambush twice a week if Lucius hadn't been riding with me.

"I've never seen anybody so good at getting inside the other guy's brain. He could dope out what a holed-up gunman was going to do five miles before we ever got to the hideout.

"Then he met this Martha. She's a great lady now, but let me tell you something. I know Becky wanted to talk to you; I'll bet it was about keeping her 'past' quiet, as if that mattered a curse."

He held up a hand. "No, you don't have to say anything or jeopardize any promise you might have made. Hell, I care more about Becky than if she was my own first flesh and blood."

"She's in love with you, you know," I said quietly.

"Hah!" Blacke slapped the table. "Don't be a bigger fool than you have to be. Sure, we're friends, but in *love* with me? I'm an old man, dead from the waist down. It makes no sense for a young gal like Becky to waste any love on me."

"If love made sense," I told him, "it wouldn't cause so much trouble."

He leveled the famous Lobo Blacke Gaze at me, the one that had backed down more criminals than a lot of other lawmen's guns had.

"Booker, do you want to talk sense, or do you want to keep embarrassing yourself with nonsense?"

I suppressed a smile. "Sense, by all means," I said. "Sorry I interrupted."

He harrumphed and said, "I guess so." Then he went on. "All I wanted to say was that Martha Jenkins's past makes Becky's past look like a convent upbringing. They used to call her three-way Martha, want to know why?"

"I think I can guess."

"Yeah, I bet you can. But that didn't make any difference to Lucius. He was in love. Now, in fairness to Martha, she was ready enough to give it up. Far as I know, since the wedding—I stood up for Lucius, by the way, before he came north—she hasn't touched another man."

Blacke's torso shook with a laugh. "Hell, as far as the evidence goes, she might not have touched Lucius but the once. And even then just one way. There is Abigail, after all."

"I don't see anything in this that's going to get your old friend hanged."

"I didn't either, for years. But I started seeing things, and hearing things from other marshals. Bandits pulling jobs they weren't smart enough to plan; fancy lawyers appearing from nowhere to get some two-bit bushwhacker off. I started making notes, and I could see a consistency behind it all. One mind. A mind that worked a lot like Lucius's."

"But no evidence."

"Not a scrap. And I don't have any today. But I've got a couple of little facts that sit in my mind and irritate it all day long, like an itch you can't reach.

"One—Lucius has made a fortune."

"We know that. In cattle and wheat and mining—"

"And sheep, too," Blacke said. "And everything else you can make money with in this country. Hardly seems natural for the same man to run cattle and sheep, but Lucius has done it. And not only has he done it, he's made it pay. And not only has he made it pay, he's had no trouble from the cattlemen or the sheepmen."

"Meaning he might have something on them?"

"Meaning whatever the reason, he's pulled off a goddam miracle."

"Is that your fact?"

"No, but now that we come to think of it, it's suggestive, isn't it? Here's the fact: Lucius has made all this money without *borrowing a dime*. He started from nothing, but he always had cash to pay for anything he bought."

"His payoffs for planning crimes?" I mused. "Could be. What's your other fact?"

"The other fact is that the night I was shot, I was on my way to talk to Kenny Abeliene, an old puncher from Texas Lucius and I both knew from the old days. He had something to tell me, something very important. So important, he would meet me in a room in downtown Boulder. Hell, Kenny never came into a town from one year to the next, but he knew something about the K and A gold robbery, and he was going to tell me and only me."

The K&A Railroad had lost almost two hundred thousand in gold in a daring raid about five years ago. The bandits killed six railroad employees and six passengers, including a woman and a little boy, in the process.

"Well, I went," Blacke said. "And Kenny opened the door. And I went inside. Then the lights went out and I was hit on the head."

"In that order?" I asked.

Blacke smiled. "I was right about you," he said. "You are a sly one. Yeah, in that order. Means it was a trap. Means there was someone else in the room.

"And when I came to, I saw that this someone else had drilled Kenny right between the eyes. But this same someone rolled me over on my belly, and put the muzzle of a pistol against my spine and pulled the trigger."

I rubbed my chin, then stopped when I realized that was one of Blacke's pet gestures. I was only working for the man, I didn't want to become him.

"Couldn't have you poking around anymore," I mused, "but didn't have the heart to flat-out kill you."

"Or wanted me to suffer more. I'd been asking a few questions; maybe I wasn't sufficiently discreet, as you might put it. He's got a mind, maybe he put two and two together. And true, maybe in honor of our old friendship, he decided just to cripple me and not to kill me.

"Or maybe over the years, he's done so much evil that it was fun for him to think of me suspecting him while I was living on charity, getting bedsores and unable to do anything about it."

He pushed back and took another of his deep breaths.

"Then you came along, Booker, and changed all that. You couldn't give me back my legs, but you gave me back my dignity."

"I gave you nothing, Mr. Blacke. I'm still collecting half the profits on your life, you know. We've both earned our share."

"I know what I know, Booker. We don't have to dwell on it. That kind of talk isn't easy for me, anyway.

"But during that time we were working on that book, I got to know you. You're shrewd, and you're tough, and maybe, in your way, smart as Lucius, but that doesn't matter anymore, because I am, too. Now I am, anyway. When you can't use your body, your mind pumps up to take up the slack. If you've got one at all, that is."

"The modesty worked very well in the book, but it's not necessary with me."

He chuckled. "Well, it's good to practice. I want to be underestimated." His smile was replaced by a scowl.

"That's the trouble," he said. "I wanted you to be underestimated, too."

"Why?"

"Because, son, until you beat up two of the nastiest bastards in this territory, there wasn't anybody around here who would have treated you seriously. You could have wandered around, talked to people, acted eastern and stupid, and made more progress than I could have in years. Hell, you could have spent half your time at Lucius's house. The wife and daughter would eat you up with a spoon, with your New York accent and sophisticated ways. They might still, but it won't be the same."

"You should have told me," I said.

"I was going to tell you. I figured you could make it off the train and down the street without ruining everything."

"I've very sorry," I said stiffly. "Does this mean you want me to go?"

"What the hell are you talking about? Of *course* I don't want you to go. It's not your fault, just a tough break for me and my plan."

He leaned forward and fixed me with his eyes.

"Look," he said. "I'm not just after revenge for my legs. If Lucius Jenkins is what I think he is, he's responsible for dozens of murders, maybe over a hundred. He maybe didn't pull the trigger on all of them, but if he planned the crimes and took a share of the loot, he's as guilty as any of them. I'd like to have your help."

This time I smiled. "That's better," I said. "What do I do?"

He shrugged. "We'll just have to play it by ear. Get out, meet people, especially people associated with Jenkins, the wife and the daughter and that English knight or whatever they've got staying out there. If you can't be underrated, be mysterious. Let on you know more than you do. Maybe make people think you're an operator with angles of your own."

"I can do that," I said. "What English knight?"

"Been there almost half a year. It was in the *Witness* a few weeks ago."

"Good, I plan to go through the morgue as soon as I can."

"How about right away? I've got to go and get my damned legs massaged. Doesn't seem fair that they should take up so much work after you can't use them anymore, does it?" He wheeled himself off to his private rooms and called for Becky.

The invitation to the party at Mrs. Jenkins's house came before night had fully fallen.

So now, Saturday night, here I was, and Martha Jenkins was showing no sign of knowing that I had the ability or even the inclination to give ruffians streetside etiquette lessons.

At least I thought so until she raised her voice and said, "Everyone, please meet Mr. Quinn Booker, from New York. Mr. Booker is the one who reduced my husband's terrible bodyguards to jelly."

She gave a jolly little laugh, while everyone else looked at me as if I were an exhibit at Barnum's circus.

So it was to be plan B, formidable and mysterious, after all.

6

LUCIUS JENKINS WAS mostly missing from his own party. I had seen him only once. He had entered grumbling, had a glass of champagne, and left.

I spent much of the evening getting to know the daughter. Blacke had a real genius as an assignment editor; he knew how to make a reporter happy.

Abigail Jenkins was smaller than her mother, below average height, and she was a true beauty, with black hair and flashing black eyes to match, a skin smooth and clear, with no need of her mother's kohl and rouge and powder.

When I danced with her (music provided by two fiddles and a guitar; they were fine, but Martha Jenkins winced whenever the musicians tried to sing), I could feel that her figure was her own, unenhanced by padding, unencumbered by whalebone.

The party was in honor of what passed for the local gentry—the town lawyer, the railroad agent, neighboring ranchers, and their families. They looked uniformly uncomfortable, but dared not refuse, since to one extent or another, all their livelihoods depended on the goodwill of Lucius Jenkins.

I was not unfamiliar with that kind of power. My grandfather wielded it over a number of people in New York. It was the kind of power he wanted to hand on to me. I can't imagine anyone actually wanting it, though I know that men do. I know that throughout history, men have killed to get it.

But while the bulk of the guests at the party might not be having a good time, there were two who definitely were—Martha Jenkins and Professor Edward Belking Vessemer.

I mentioned my observation to Abigail.

"Mother is a queen bee," she said. Her voice was quite girlish. Considering her eighteen years, and the undoubted maturity of her face and form, it made one suspect that she was feigning, but it was simply one of the mismatches that nature sometimes creates.

"The town is her hive, and the drones and workers move as she moves."

"Very perceptive," I said.

"You dance very well," she said.

"Don't change the subject."

"Oh, but that's my prerogative, isn't it? As a woman, I mean? Tell me about your adventures."

"You wouldn't want to hear my adventures," I said. Besides, I thought, she couldn't. I really hadn't had any. But I was being formidable and mysterious, so I let it go at that.

"You are wrong, Mr. Booker. We have done virtually nothing for the past three days but speculate about you, and wonder at how you bested Frank and Marvin. Father was horribly vexed with them."

"For insulting a lady?" I asked.

"For not beating you senseless. They're supposed to be his bodyguards, you know."

"Does your father truly require bodyguards?"

"He thinks he does. I expect every powerful man thinks he does. Or wants to. What good does it do to be powerful, if you can't wallow in the jealousy of lesser men?"

"You are very young to be jaded."

"On the contrary, Mr. Booker. I am not at all jaded. I love being the daughter of Lucius Jenkins. I come closer to doing exactly what I please than anyone I ever heard of."

"And what might that be?"

She half closed her eyes and laughed deep in her throat. "You just might find that out before too long, Mr. Booker, if you play your cards right."

A sudden, sharp, animal reaction surprised and alarmed me. I was aware of her attractions but hadn't realized how much the instinctual me wanted her.

I forced myself to control my face. Very calmly, I said, "Don't forget that you have a hand to play, too, my dear."

"Of course. It's what makes the game worthwhile, isn't it? The cut and thrust?"

I looked at her. Her face was serene, but her eyes were laughing.

Before I could say more, the music came to an end.

"Please excuse me," I said. "I hope to speak to you again, later."

"I'll never forgive you if you don't." She walked away, looking back once coyly over her shoulder at me.

I desired to speak with Vessemer. He was hard to find in the crowd and the dim light, but somehow, his cigar smoke was whiter and thicker than everyone else's, and I found him at the bottom of a plume of it.

He had a glass of something brown in his hand and sipped it occasionally with his eyes closed. When he did, his smile got even more beatific.

"I'm glad you're enjoying yourself, Professor."

"Ah, Booker, how can anyone who appreciates human behavior fail to enjoy himself at a gathering like this? The fears, the tensions, the hatreds and infatuations. Fascinating. I wish I could somehow photograph it."

"I'd like to talk to you about a photograph," I said.

"I'll be delighted to take your photograph," he said. "At a special rate, in honor of the talks we had on the train."

"Thank you, Professor, but no. Neither my vanity nor my sense of history are well enough developed."

He removed his cigar long enough to grin at me.

"Pity," he said.

"I'm talking about the photograph I had you take the other day. You still haven't asked me for payment."

"That one," he said, "was on the house. I shall be in Le Four until Wednesday. Give me a few hours' notice, and you may pick up a print at any time."

"That won't be necessary," I said. "Young Marvin made such a piteous spectacle of himself outside the house this evening that I told him I wouldn't show Miss Abigail the photograph. Apparently he worships her from afar."

He looked away from me and around the room. I tracked his gaze until I saw that he was watching Abigail Jenkins dancing with Sir Peter

Melling. The Englishman was talking earnestly in the young woman's ear; she in turn wore a dismissive smile. I had seen the steps to that particular dance a hundred times; had performed them myself once or twice. The man was earnestly attempting to make love to the lady; she was distantly amused, but was by societal rules obliged to put up with his attentions.

I truly might as well have been back in New York.

"From afar," the professor said, meeting my eyes once more. "Some do it in greater proximity."

I smiled at the joke.

He went on. "You offered this promise, I suppose, in exchange for one of future good behavior?"

"That's right."

"You should keep a copy of the photograph to assure compliance."

He was right. I should. Thinking back, I realized I hadn't promised I wouldn't keep a copy, just that I wouldn't show it to Abigail.

"You're right. He seemed genuinely contrite, but this is a young man who comes with the bad companions attached. I'll pick up a copy on Monday."

"You can visit tomorrow, if you'd like to. The only reason I don't do business on Sunday is that it might scandalize the townspeople."

"All right. I'll come by tomorrow afternoon after dinner. Oh, and I also promised Marvin I'd ask you not to show the photograph to Miss Abigail, either."

"He asked me that himself when I arrived. I gave him no definite answer."

"Well, as a favor to me."

"As a favor to you, I'll oblige." He took a big puff on his cigar. He'd have to light another one soon; this one was down to a stub. "But don't tell Marvin. I have been small and slight all my life, and I don't like bullies, no matter whose thumb they're under. It amuses me to see him uncomfortable and to know I'm the cause of it. Allow me to indulge myself during my few remaining days in this town."

"Certainly," I said. I was about to add more when I saw Martha Jenkins looming down on us like a ship of the line with a smaller vessel in tow.

In fact, he wasn't smaller at all; he was bluff and wind burned, blond and hearty, and an inch or two taller than Mrs. Jenkins.

"Pardon me for interrupting, gentlemen," she said, "but there is someone else I'd like you to meet."

She proceeded to present us to Sir Peter Melling, Baronet. This was the "English knight or something" Blacke had referred to.

Blacke had known better. His error had been a way of suggesting I check the newspaper's files, which I would have done anyway.

The files were full of Sir Peter. The baronet had come to Le Four to explore the possibility of buying property here, since he had grown tired of the unsettled ways of European Society. He was forty years old and unmarried, and was staying at the home of his friend, Lucius Jenkins, with whom he had had some trans-Atlantic business dealings in the past.

That had been back in April, so the baronet had apparently settled in for a good, long visit. Having seen him dancing with Abigail before, I suspected I knew the reason.

He shook our hands firmly and was delighted to meet us.

"Our hostess has been telling me all about you," he said. "About both of you. And of course, Professor, like every cultured person with an interest in the West, I am familiar with your work."

Vessemer made a little bow, but he never took his eyes off the Englishman's face.

Sir Peter went on to say that while the West was a wonderful place of unlimited opportunity, it seemed to be culturally barren at times.

"It's still young," I said.

"Very true. Part of its charm, in fact. Still it is, as our hostess would say, a rare pleasure to meet such cultured men as yourselves in such a place. Raises the tone."

He went on to ask me if I was related to Lord Booker of Hampshire.

"Not that I know of," I told him. "Just Colonel Booker of West Point. I didn't even know there was a Lord Booker."

"Oh, yes," Sir Peter said. "Since the fifteenth century, I think. Possibly the sixteenth."

"Fascinating," I said. "The next time I'm in your country I'll look him up."

"Oh, have you been to England?"

"Once or twice," I told him.

So we talked about England. I must admit that I had my suspicions of him—adopting a foreign persona to impress a snob of a mother and get close to the heiress daughter struck me as just the sort of Buncombe game that would be especially suited to *nouveau riche* in any locality, but especially in a place like Le Four wherein the *nouveau riche* had no opportunity to learn from watching the *riche vieux* because the *nouveau* variety were the only *riche* around.

After twenty minutes of talking, all I could say was that if Sir Peter Melling was a fraud, he was a good one. His accent and manner were right, and his details were right as far as I knew them from my own experience.

And he had some well-developed manners, too.

All the time we were talking, Professor Ned was frankly staring at the Englishman. I assumed that as a photographer he took a professional interest in faces, and although the baronet's red, lined, and monocled visage was something to see, it still seemed a mite excessive.

It would have unsettled me, I'm sure. In fact, I remembered being mildly unsettled by the relatively mild scrutiny the photographer had subjected my own face to on the train that brought us here.

But aside from a few pointed looks, Sir Peter reacted not at all to the professor's rudeness. I remember thinking the man had remarkable self-control.

He did mention it after the professor took a watch out of his pocket and said he really must get his horse and get back to town.

"If I don't have it at Blanc's by nine tomorrow morning, the bandit will charge me for another day."

"Are you a horseman, then, sir?" the baronet asked.

"I love it," the professor replied. He took a puff on his cigar; the look he gave Sir Peter was still one of more than normal interest, but the obsessiveness was gone. "Even on a cold winter night," he said. "I spend so much time on trains, a good canter is like a vacation to me. I wouldn't ride in a carriage if I could. Do you ride, Sir Peter?"

"Not since I left England," he said. "It's ironic, I know, to have visited America at last, to the Great American West, and not to have had a chance to sit a horse for six months, but I injured my leg shortly after arriving, and since it healed have been battling gout. That is part of the reason I have imposed on poor Mrs. Jenkins's hospitality for so long."

"I doubt she sees it as an imposition," said the professor dryly.

There was something almost impish in Sir Peter's grin. "She is a very gracious lady, with an exaggerated idea of the luster of a trumpery little baronetcy such as my own. At any rate, I was delighted simply to be able to manage to dance, however clumsily, with Mrs. Jenkins and Miss Abigail tonight. That about does it for me. Soon I'll be limping off to bed."

"Yes!" the professor said. "And I must be off to town. I'll see you tomorrow, then, Booker?"

"Yes. I can't give you a precise time; I don't know when Mrs. Sundberg serves Sunday dinner."

"It doesn't matter. I shall be in my Pullman all day." He shook my hand, then the Englishman's. "Sir Peter," he said. "If you find yourself in town anytime before Wednesday, I should like very much to photograph you. You are a new breed of settler to the West—the elite of the Old World eager to face the challenge of the New—and I would like to add you to my photographic record of the people of this land."

Sir Peter said he was flattered and would make every effort to get to the professor's rolling studio.

"Fascinating man," the baronet observed as the professor left us.

"Very much so."

"I—er—I saw you dancing with Miss Abigail," he said. "You dance quite well."

I smiled ruefully. "It was drilled into me as diligently as close-order drill to a soldier. And I have been fortunate enough to have been spared broken legs and gout."

"She seemed quite taken with you."

"She was merely gracious." I lied. She was something, all right, but it had little to do with grace.

"She has great spirit."

I said that as far as could be decided on a short acquaintance, I agreed with him.

"I have grown very fond of her," he told me. "Very protective."

It suddenly dawned on me what he was driving at, and I had to control my face to suppress astonishment. Here was a titled Englishman concerned with *me* as a rival suitor. My grandmother would have been in ecstasy.

"I'm sure she appreciates that." I lied again. It seemed to mollify him. He walked off, not quite limping, and left the party.

The conversation ended; I mingled with the rest of the guests, collecting names and comments (Blacke would want a story on this do for the *Witness*) for another hour or so, then thanked my hostess and her daughter ("We must have that card game soon, Mr. Booker," she told me at parting) and left.

I was sure I would dream about her that night, but I was wrong.

7

THE HIGHWAYMAN ATTACKED us about two miles out of town.

He emerged from a clump of winter-dead bushes thirty yards from the frozen roadway on a black horse, dressed all in black, with a flour-sack hood hiding his face. If he'd emerged from his hiding place a few seconds sooner, he could have cut off our advance with ease and had his way with us. Instead, he waited too long and gave Sundberg a chance to whip the horses to a gallop and shoot our carriage ahead of the attacker.

I didn't take this all in at the time. I saw the horse; I heard Sundberg curse and crack the whip. I was thrown back against the seat by the sudden acceleration.

It wasn't until I looked back at our pursuer and saw the orange blossoms of flame erupt from his hand and heard the crack of the gunshots that I put together what was happening.

Damn, I thought absurdly. I'm going to have to start carrying a gun after all.

If I'd had one, I would have had a decent chance of dealing with the attacker, because he was a pitiful shot. None of his bullets came close to us, so far as I could tell; they simply amplified the effect of Sundberg's whip on the horse and spurred the animal to even greater speed. The carriage bounced crazily on the frozen ruts of the road, nearly upsetting us several times.

Our horse ran fast, but the horse behind us, unencumbered with equipage, ran faster and gained on us. Soon the highwayman was alongside us, on our left. He was close enough to reach out his right hand, pull the trigger, and blow off Sundberg's head or mine at point-blank range.

Even as I muttered a last prayer, I wondered what this madman was hoping to accomplish. This was no stagecoach, laden with gold for banks in the West. This was a private carriage with two working men inside. I didn't know how much Sundberg was carrying on him, but from my body the thief could count on a gold eagle and perhaps three more dollars in smaller coins, plus my watch.

I knew it was hopeless, but I tried to make myself small, hoping he would run out of bullets or something before he killed me.

But the shot never came. He never shot at Sundberg, either. Instead, he continued to gallop until he was even with our horse. Sundberg tried to get our animal to swerve into his and perhaps unseat him, but when he did, the carriage tilted precariously on one wheel, nearly unseating us.

If I had been driving, I might have reined in and let the attacker go shooting past. It wouldn't have done much good—there was really no place for us to go, and the horseman would wheel and catch up with us in seconds, but in those few seconds we might have been able to split up and flee on foot. Anything would be better than this desperate race we could not win.

That we had, in fact, already lost. I began screaming over to Sundberg over the rush of the wind and the pounding of hoofbeats that he should stop the wagon, but it was too late.

Our attacker reached down to his saddle and drew something from the rifle scabbard that was not a rifle. Instead, it appeared to be a thin straight stick, about three feet long. I don't know what I expected him to do with it, but I know what he did.

He reached across and poked our horse in the left hindquarter.

You'll forgive me if the next few moments are confused in my memory.

The horse collapsed, simply buckled where the stick had touched him. He went down and rolled off the road, taking the carriage, Sundberg, and me with it.

I was lucky—I managed to jump clear. I tried to roll as I landed on the rock-hard frozen earth, but when I stopped, I felt like an egg dropped on a tabletop.

The horse was making frightened noises in its throat. Sundberg was silent. I heard hoofbeats approaching cautiously. I didn't think he had anything to worry about.

Through slitted eyes, I looked up at him. He seemed gigantic, but then I was flat on my back on the ground, and he was on horseback. I say "he," but it could have been a woman or a demon from hell for all I knew.

Slowly, the figure walked his horse through the wreckage. I lay completely still. I'd like to let you think I was playing possum, but the truth is I was breathless and stunned and couldn't have moved more than my eyelids if I'd wanted to.

He was looming over me when he drew his gun. I willed myself to get up, to run, but nothing happened. The figure was still holding the gun at the ready when he turned his horse and swept out of my field of vision.

I heard two shots, then hoofbeats as the rider galloped away.

Then there was complete silence. He'd shot the horse and Sundberg, I thought, and left me here, paralyzed, to freeze to death.

I could feel panic setting in, and something close to despair. I forced myself to think rationally. First of all, I was not actually paralyzed. With great concentration and effort, I could move both my hands and my feet. That meant that as soon as I could muster sufficient will, I could stand, and maybe even walk.

Secondly, even if I had been paralyzed, I probably wouldn't have frozen to death. There were still guests at Jenkins's party who had to come home along this route. I would be found.

And when I was, I decided, I would be found on my feet. It hurt like nothing ever had, but I made it.

Then I concentrated on getting my legs to move, which, much to my surprise, they did. I staggered around the site of the accident.

In a way it was awesome to see. The cold had frozen the ground so hard, there were no tracks or traces of what had happened. No hoofprints. No wagon tracks. Just the destruction, as if some angry God had picked us up and dropped us to the roadside from a great height.

"Sundberg?" I said. Not expecting an answer, and getting none, I looked for him, and found him under the wreckage of the buckboard with his head knocked back and sideways in a position impossible for a living man. I closed my eyes and shook my head. I hadn't known him long, but I'd liked him.

And someone was going to have to tell his wife.

The horse's leg was bent at an improbable angle, and it was the horse on which the highwayman had used the two bullets.

How humane, I thought. What a very humane bastard this killer must be.

I didn't want to stay there; every time I looked at poor Sundberg, my gorge would rise with anger, and I would start to shake. I needed something purposeful to do, something that would take all my concentration to achieve.

I took a deep breath, gathered my greatcoat around me, and forced my bruised and aching legs to take me down the rutted road toward town.

If any astronomer wishes to know what the dark side of the moon is like, he may apply to me, because I fancy my walk took me there. It was certainly no earthly experience. It was bleak and barren, as if the sun had never shone there nor ever would, and the wind was a thin, cold whisper because of it. I was the only life, staggering along helplessly forever, because I could think of nothing better to do.

That illusion lasted about a mile and a half, until I found the body.

I did not know who it was at first. I just thought it was another victim.

"The highwayman has been busy tonight," I said.

I jumped when I heard myself. I was surprised to find that my voice worked.

The body lay athwart the road about a hundred yards ahead when I first saw it in the darkness. I even managed the grotesque parody of a run in order to get to it the sooner, in case I could be of help.

Two small holes in the back told me that no amount of running would have helped. I rolled the smallish body over and saw the bearded face of Professor Edward Vessemer.

I sat and cursed. I might have screamed. I might have cried; mercifully, my mind has blotted out the memory of the next few minutes. I simply know that I at last got myself back to my feet again and headed toward town with a grim determination. I was already vowing to do something about what had happened tonight.

And my legs hardly hurt at all.

8

SHERIFF ASA HARLAN reached inside his shirt and scratched his ample belly.

"Don't get riled up, Blacke," he said. "I got to ask these questions, and you know it."

The sheriff's voice was querulous and impatient. Murders had happened in his jurisdiction last night, assaults, and (since the horse the professor had been riding had yet to be found) probable horse theft, but the worst thing that happened was that he had been dragged out of bed at three A.M. He couldn't just now lay hands on the perpetrators, and if Blacke's opinion of him was to be believed, he never would.

But I was the one who had caused him to be awakened, and I was right here, and by damn, one way or another, I was going to pay for it.

"I know you've got to ask questions," Blacke replied. "Somebody told you that that's what a lawman is supposed to do, and you do it. I just wish they'd told you why."

"You're always doing that," the sheriff complained. He scratched himself some more. "You're always insulting me, in person and in that stupid newspaper of yours."

Blacke raised an eyebrow. "Got someone reading it to you, have you?"

"See? You're doing it again. I can read. I can read as good as anybody. Ain't this a peaceable town? Don't I do a good job? Why are you always treating me like an idjit?"

"Because you act like an idiot. A witness and a victim walks up to your door to report a crime, takes you to the scene, and tells you what happened, and what do you do? You clap him in that cell over there."

Blacke pointed over the sheriff's shoulder to where I stood behind the bars. Harlan looked back over his shoulder at the indication.

"Still here, Sheriff," I said pleasantly. When he turned back, I made a face at him and almost succeeded in making Rebecca, standing behind Blacke's wheelchair, lose her earnest and self-effacing demeanor and crack a smile. Not quite, but close.

Harlan started ticking off points on his stubby fingers.

"One," he began.

"Good start," Blacke told him.

I could see the muscles tighten in the back of his neck, and the bald spot above the untidy gray wool that fringed it turn red, but he didn't allow himself to get distracted.

"One," he said again, "this Booker is a stranger in town. Two. He admits he was out there. Three, there's no proof nobody but him was *ever* out there. Except the dead men, of course. No tracks of man nor horse, nothing dropped at the scenes that doesn't belong to Booker or to one of the dead men."

Harlan folded his arms across his chest and nodded his head for punctuation.

Blacke spoke quietly. "Are you done?"

"I'm done."

"There are plenty of numbers left," Blacke suggested. "I'll bet you can count all the way to twenty."

"Get to the point, dammit, or I'll throw you out of here, wheelchair or no wheelchair."

Blacke showed him a tight grin.

"You try it," he said, "and I'll bust you in half. Wheelchair or no wheelchair."

"Uncle Louis," Rebecca chided him. I could see she wasn't too wild about the idea of Blacke engaging in rough business. I found it fairly appalling myself.

However stupid Harlan was—and on my brief acquaintance I had detected a stupidity both profound and tenacious—he was not stupid enough to get physical with a crippled man who was at once the publisher of the town newspaper and a beloved legend of the West.

"I said I was done," he reiterated. Then he said, "No, I'm not, either. I was saving this, but what the hell.

"Your friend here says the killer was a highwayman, right? Well, in your long experience as a lawman, Blacke, I'm sure you know that highwaymen sometimes kill, but one thing they don't do. *They don't forget to rob the victims.* Booker already admits the man didn't take nothing from him or Sundberg, and the professor was found with almost fifty dollars in his pocket."

I made a noise.

The sheriff wheeled on me, and I was treated to another look at his big round red face with the tiny blue eyes and the button nose with the huge, woolly gray moustache beneath it hiding the mouth completely.

"You say something, Booker?" he demanded.

"No, sir," I said. "Something stuck in my throat."

That was true. What had stuck there was my suspicion that when the sheriff found the professor's body, there had probably been a lot more than fifty dollars on it. I had to console myself with the vision of how it must have pained him to leave the rest of the money behind. I was sort of proud that the idea of having an excuse to arrest me was worth fifty dollars to him.

Now Blacke pushed his hat back on his forehead with his thumb and looked up at Harlan.

He began ticking points off on his own fingers.

"One," he said. "Booker may be a stranger in Le Four, but I've known him for four years. Not only does he come from a prominent and wealthy family back east, he is my partner in a very successful business venture. Just by coming here, he became one of the richest men in town, behind Jenkins and me and possibly you, depending on how much Jenkins slips you under the table each month."

The bald spot glowed bright red.

"You take that back!" the sheriff demanded.

Blacke ignored him. "So I vouch for him completely; I wouldn't work with him if he couldn't be trusted."

You can ask Jenkins about that, I thought.

"He has no reason whatever to hurt Sundberg or Professor Ned."

"That we know of," Harlan said.

"Two. You say he admits he was out there, as though you're proving something. You'd have a damn sight more to be suspicious about if he tried to claim he *wasn't* out there. He was invited to the party at Jenkins's place, and he went. Dozens of people saw him there. He left the party to come home, and that's the only road that goes between town and Bellevue."

Harlan was sulky. "There's trails. Plenty of them."

"He was in a *buckboard*, Asa. With Sundberg, remember? My friend and employee whom you claim Booker killed. Remember him?"

"I remember him. Your other friend and employee here killed him."

"And the professor?"

"Him too."

"Shot him, you say?"

"Twice in the back."

"Well, Harlan, that would be a good trick, wouldn't it? Where's the gun? Booker doesn't go around armed—"

"I will from now on, by God," I put in. I had assumed an air of flippancy when that "idjit" of a sheriff put me under arrest because I knew it was the best way to keep him off balance. Now that Blacke had the situation more or less under control, though, my emotions were beginning to dwell on the realization that two good men had been killed tonight, and it might have been three if I hadn't been too stunned to move. The killer had apparently decided that like Sundberg, I had been killed in the fall, and decided to save the ammunition.

"Don't interrupt," Blacke told me. "It confuses the sheriff."

He turned his attention back to Harlan. "Booker doesn't go armed. Sundberg's religion wouldn't let him touch a gun. And the professor had a derringer in his pocket, which you already told me was found there, both rounds in it, unfired."

"So?"

Blacke pounded a fist into the arm of his wheelchair. "So *how in blazes did the two forty-five slugs get into Vessemer?* And back out again for that matter? Do you think Booker here *spit* them at the man?"

"Now look—"

Blacke gave him no chance to speak.

"Was this supposed to be before or after he made the buckboard crash—with himself inside it? You've had his sleeves rolled up—do those bruises look like the kind that a man could give himself?"

Harlan was puzzled. "Why would a man want to give bruises to him*self*?"

Blacke rolled his eyes. "Never mind. The fact is, Booker is hurt plenty. As soon as you let him out of there, I'm taking him next door to Doc Mayhew's place and wake him up."

"I'm not letting him out of no place."

Blacke went red in the face and planted his hands on the arms of his wheelchair as if wishing to God he could stand up and pound Harlan's face for him.

"*You* look. When I walk—when I go through that door, I'm going to have one of two destinations. I'm either bringing Booker to the doctor, or I'm going back to the office to start setting type for an extra edition of the *Witness*, detailing the crime and your mishandling of it. Then I won't be the only one who knows what a fool you are, Harlan—everybody will know it. And they'll wonder what a smart man like Lucius Jenkins is doing propping you up."

That did the trick. Despite his bluster, Harlan didn't mind people thinking he was an idiot. He couldn't have minded that and lived, since, I learned as my days in Le Four stretched on, *everybody* thought so. Because he *was* an idiot. Even Harlan must have been dimly aware of that.

But if one idea was sharp and clear below the wool and skin and bone of his head, it was that *Jenkins must never be embarrassed.* For Asa Harlan, Lucius Jenkins was the source of all good things. If Jenkins tired of the sheriff, he would be sheriff no more. He would be forced to seek employment suitable to his talents, like shoveling out stables.

He must have been reviewing all this in the dim privacy of his mind, because his bald spot glowed bright red with the effort of it. The shine approached incandescence.

I watched in fascination. Just as I expected it to start to smoke, the sheriff spoke.

"Don't be so hasty, Blacke. You got the worst temper, sometimes."

"Sometimes," Blacke said, "I get provoked."

"Well, then," Harlan said. His moustache stretched in a smile. "No sense in getting ourselves all riled. You make some good points, now, come to think of it. I'm gonna deputize some men and get them looking for that gun."

For a minute, I thought Blacke was going to tell him all the things wrong with that idea, from the fact that unless I had done it, there wouldn't be any gun hidden out there to the fact that finding a gun on the road wouldn't prove anything against me or anyone else unless he could find the bullets, too.

Blacke went so far as to open his mouth. Then he saw the futility of it and closed it again. He swallowed hard, then said, "You do that, Sheriff."

"In the meantime, you vouch for young Booker, here?"

"One hundred percent."

"Then I don't really have no call to keep him locked up. Busted up the way he is it wouldn't be *humane*."

He turned around to let me see the grin. He was delighted with himself for having come up with the word.

"Good," Blacke said. "Now unlock the door and let him go."

"Yeah. Now, you won't go off half-cocked in that newspaper of yours, will you?"

"I never do, Harlan."

The sheriff decided that was the best promise he was going to get, so he took the keys, clanked the lock open, and let me loose. I'd been standing in one place so long my bruised muscles had stiffened and I could hardly walk. Each step took concentration and effort, but I was damned if I was going to let Sheriff Harlan offer me an arm.

I looked around for my hat, then realized it was back on the prairie somewhere. I walked stiff-legged across the wooden floor, certain I was going to collapse. When I got to Blacke, I told Rebecca I'd push the wheelchair.

"Oh, Mr. Booker, you don't need to do—"

I whispered to her, "I need something to lean on." Blacke overheard and cracked a broad grin.

Once we were out on the boardwalk, Blacke looked at me critically. "You do look bad, Booker. Maybe worse than I thought. Let's get to the doctor right away."

"You think I'm going to be tough and argue with you, don't you?"

"I think you're going to be smart and do what I say."

"Right as usual, Mr. Blacke," I said. "Which way?"

"Two doors to the left. Maybe I should get out of the chair and let you sit."

"Don't tempt me," I told him.

Rebecca pointed out that the cold night air could not be helping my condition. I leaned on the handles of the wheelchair and limped off in the proper direction. Rebecca took my arm. To her, I had no objection. It felt nice.

Blacke talked back over his shoulder. "Can you talk? Can you think?"

"Seems to me I can."

"That's no help. It probably seems to Harlan that he can, too. He's such a fool, he didn't remember we won't need to wake up Mayhew."

"I don't want to look like a tenderfoot or anything, but—" A bolt of pain passed through my body like a streak of lightning. When I caught my breath, I said, "But I really think I ought to see him."

"You'll see him. I just meant he's awake, because he's the coroner.

"I want a look at those bodies," he said.

9

O NCE I'D BEEN pointed in the right direction, I had no problem. Doc Mayhew's place was hard to miss. For one thing, his name was painted all over his windows in buff, red, and black, and he had a sign out over the street in the same colors proclaiming:

HECTOR MAYHEW (M.D., Ph.D.) MEDICAL CLINIC
Expert Treatment of All Diseases and Conditions of Ill Health
Gunshot Wounds a Specialty
Sovereign Remedies Expertly Compounded on Premises
Recognized by All National and International Medical Societies

I imagined one of my grandmother's Fifth Avenue doctors seeing that sign and passing out on the spot from indignation. Personally, I like a man who has pride in his work.

Light spilled from the windows; the door was unlocked. Rebecca held it open while I wheeled Blacke inside. There was a bell to ring, but Blacke preferred to use his lungs.

"Doc Mayhew!" he bellowed. "It's Louis Blacke! I've got a patient for you, a live one this time!"

Blacke turned to me. "When he gets interested in something in the back room, he ignores the bell. Hadn't you better sit down?"

"Nothing would delight me more," I said. "But once I sit, I'm not too sure of being able to get up again."

Doctor Mayhew came out. He was nothing like what the sign had led me to imagine. I'd been expecting a small, bombastic man with the slick patter of the medicine-show barker.

Instead, he resembled a bearded stork. He was very tall, maybe six and a half feet, and very lean, almost emaciated. Where the straight, mouse brown beard didn't hide his face, you could almost see the man's skull. His skin was so tight, creases marked the full circle of his eyeballs behind wire-framed spectacles.

He came to us at a near run, the flapping of the white tails of his working smock enhancing his resemblance to the long-legged bird. A long, thin beak of a nose helped too.

His arrival was anticipated by an atmosphere—a distinctive, clean smell.

I could, as it were, hardly believe my nose.

I sniffed. "Carbolic?" I asked.

He beamed. "You recognize it?"

"I do."

"And you know what I use it for?"

"Asepsis in medical procedure," I answered.

He took my hand and pumped it wildly. "Excellent," he said. "Are you by chance a physician?"

"The grandson of a neuraesthenic woman," I replied. "That can be a medical education in itself."

He laughed but didn't let go of my hand. The pumping started to hurt. I disengaged as well as I could.

Blacke was irritable. "What the hell are you talking about?" he demanded.

"Modern medical science," Mayhew told him. "Dr. Pasteur of Paris has shown that infection can be caused by tiny animals too small to be seen by the naked eye; Dr. Lister of Vienna has shown that boiling medical linen and instruments and washing hands and other instruments in dilute carbolic acid kills these organisms and prevents infection. That is why so many more of my gunshot patients live compared to those who visit other practitioners. I cannot convince my colleagues in the territory to bathe the wounds daily in carbolic solution and let the body heal itself."

"Acid on a gunshot wound? It must hurt."

"As one who has tried it on my own minor wounds, I must tell you it hurts almost beyond imagining. But I am convinced it spells the difference between life and the lingering death of sepsis."

"Well," Blacke said, "you're the doctor."

"Indeed. And who is the patient?" Before I could answer, he went on, "Or are you here about the remains of Mr. Sundberg?"

Blacke nodded. "I want to see his body. The professor's, too, but—"

"I strongly advise against it. They are not prepared for viewing—that is not my field of expertise. When I am done, I shall release the body to the undertaker, but in the meantime—"

"I want to see the bodies, Doctor, because I've got some ideas about the murders, and you know the sheriff is going to be useless."

"I have known that," Mayhew intoned, "for some time."

"All right, then. But I'm trying to tell you, you do have a patient."

"Yes?"

Blacke hooked a thumb at me. "This young man. Dr. Booker of New York. He was thrown from a buckboard traveling at high speed to frozen ground."

"But that's what happened to Sundberg!"

"I know," I said. "I was traveling with him."

"You must be in great pain," the doctor said. There was real concern in his voice.

"He's only standing up because he's afraid to sit," Blacke said.

Doctor Mayhew peered down his nose at me. "The dead can wait. You come with me."

He brought me into a small room and had me take off my clothes. I looked myself over as the doctor did.

From a strictly visual point of view, I was better than I thought. It was true that I had bruises that rivaled in size, shape, and color the designs on the doctor's wallpaper, and something that looked like a map of the Dakota Territory along my side, complete with swellings to represent the Black Hills, but no parts were hanging off me, and aside from a few scrapes, most of my skin remained intact.

Doctor Mayhew palpated my abdomen and my back, arms, and legs. Almost unique in my experience of doctors, he did this in silence. No little hums or murmurs, just strict attention to his work. I decided I could get to like the man.

Finally he finished. "You," he said, "are a very lucky man."

"I don't feel very lucky," I said as I tried to stuff stiff limbs back into my clothes.

"Are you going to join Blacke in examining the bodies?"

"Sure," I said. "I found them in the first place."

"Well, I've got Ole Sundberg stretched out on a table in the other room, and if I put you on a table beside him and told you to lie still, no one would be able to tell the difference. There *is* no difference, except that he broke his neck in the fall, and you didn't."

"I see," I said. But I was seeing something else, too. The idea that I could very well be dead at this moment—that I *would* be dead if I had happened to have landed a different way—brought home the horror of what I had seen and experienced. It was suddenly very personal to me.

I said as much to the doctor.

"That's fine," he said. "But don't let yourself get too agitated right now. Are you in the habit of taking laudanum?"

"Never."

"Good. I can prescribe a minimum dose, then. Ten drops in water. I would pour it out for you now, but I assume you wish a clear head while you examine the bodies with Blacke and me."

"Yes," I said. I would have given anything to have this pain relieved, but not only did I wish to keep a clear head, I knew that the pain was the only thing keeping me awake.

I reminded myself that just a few hours before I had been dancing to sweet music with a beautiful and flirtatious woman in my arms. It seemed impossible.

When I was dressed again, the doctor handed me an amber bottle and told me to take it back to the *Witness* with me. He'd written the instructions on the label. I should take it easy for the next couple of days, and I should be all right.

We went to rejoin Blacke.

"Where's Rebecca?" I said.

"Doc's son turned up dressed for a party and offered to walk her home. I told her to go."

Doc Mayhew's bony face smiled under his beard.

"Merton is fourteen," he said. "He's quite smitten with Miss Rebecca."

"Let's see the bodies," Blacke said.

They were in a room down the hall, a place that resembled an unholy billiard room, with the lamps suspended low over tables on which the bodies lay side by side, covered with sheets.

"I haven't begun the autopsies yet," he said apologetically. "I've just made a superficial preliminary examination. I was going to wait for daylight before I cut them open, the better to see. If you'd like to come back then . . . ?"

"No, thank you," Blacke said emphatically. "I've killed men with a gun, a knife, a rope, and a rock slide. I've seen 'em hanged, and I've been shot myself. But I can't stomach the idea of laying a dead man out on a table and cutting him apart like a saddle of beef."

"It's a source of knowledge," Mayhew said calmly. "It's a last service the dead can do the living—help us treat disease, or bring a killer to justice."

"I know that," Blacke said irritably. "I just said I didn't want to watch it. What happened to Ole?"

"Broke his neck at the second vertebra, just below the atlas," Mayhew said. "He must have landed on his head when he was thrown from the wagon. It's the same sort of injury produced in a hanging—the head snapped suddenly sideways. Nothing out of the ordinary here."

Blacke was sour. "No," he grumbled. "Just another friend of mine, dead."

"I was speaking scientifically, Louis," the doctor said.

"I know, I know. I'd be taking out my orneriness on the killer, only he doesn't happen to be here at the moment."

"Here are the contents of Mr. Sundberg's pockets."

We looked through them. Pocketknife, some small coins, nothing out of the ordinary.

"You'd think the sheriff would have collected that stuff, wouldn't you?"

Blacke turned the sour look on me. "In an ordinary town with a real sheriff you would. In Le Four, we're just as glad that idiot doesn't get his hands on things."

I reserved my assumption that he had gotten his hands on all but fifty dollars of the professor's cash. I was beginning to yearn for the laudanum.

The doctor had the professor's personal effects in a shallow wooden box, which he handed to Blacke. I looked over his shoulder as he examined the items.

Again, nothing remarkable, given Vessemer's station in life. An ivory toothpick in a gold holder. The cash. The cigar case I remembered from the train, with a full complement of six cigars in it. A letter from his wife. The sheriff had kept the derringer.

I shook my head, sadly. His wife would get a sad reply indeed to that letter.

Blacke looked intently at the cigar case, as though remembering the photographer's habit of smoking them constantly. Then he put it back in the box, handed it back to the doctor, and said, "All right, thanks."

The doctor drew back the sheet from the photographer's body. There was no dignity in the man's death. Since he'd been shot in the back, exit wounds gaped obscenely in his chest. His face was haggard and strained, and the carefully groomed hair and whiskers were all askew. The skin was now a very pale white, tinged with blue.

At that point the door opened. I jumped for my life, but it was only a lanky, thin young man, obviously the doctor's son. He had a dreamy, faraway look on his face. It was the kind of look I knew all too well from my own adolescence, when I had been allowed to spend time in the company of some older women with whom my incompetently maturing soul was besotted. I almost smiled in spite of myself.

"Father," he said respectfully, if a mite squeakily. "Gentlemen. Miss Rebecca's compliments, and she is safely home. She also said to tell you that Mrs. Sundberg is cooking."

"Cooking?"

"Yes, sir, that's what she said. I'll go back to bed now, Father."

"Not just yet, Merton. Get a smock on and help me turn the body over."

The boy's face lit up. "Do you mean it?"

"Of course I mean it, else I would not have said it."

Merton was ready in seconds. He sprang to the table and stood ready to grasp the body. Obviously, Merton's father had done a much better job of introducing his son to the charms of his profession than my father had.

"Toward me, now," the doctor said, and the boy rolled the professor's body up on its side, at which point Doctor Mayhew took over and lowered it gently again to the table, this time facedown.

The doctor pointed a bony finger to the two reddish-black holes about six inches apart on the professor's back.

"Those are the wounds caused by the bullets' entry," he said. "As you can see by their almost perfect circularity, the killer was more or less at a level with the victim when the shots were fired."

Blacke grunted and said that was consistent with his own extensive experience of bullet wounds. I was willing to take their word for it.

"Mr. Booker," the doctor said. "How much blood was there on the ground around the body?"

I closed my eyes and visualized the horrible moonlit scene again. "Virtually none," I said. "His clothes were stiff with it, though."

Merton made a face. "They sure were. I had to take them off him."

"Professor Vessemer was shot through the heart and the region around the heart. There should have been *pools* of blood around the body. And indeed, he did shed the blood. It is certainly not in his body. The obvious conclusion is that he was shot somewhere else, and the body moved to the spot on the trail at which you found it."

Blacke mumbled something. Doctor Mayhew begged his pardon.

"I said, 'Of course it was,' " Blacke nearly shouted. He took a breath and controlled his temper.

"Of course it was," he said again, more calmly. "The bullets were fired at a level. That could mean they were both on horseback, but if that had happened, the professor would have fallen from the horse to the frozen ground. He would have had some bruising. Or he would have been dragged, in which case his body would have been in even worse shape.

"But look at the body. Except for the bullet holes, there's nothing wrong with him."

"That's not—" I began.

But Blacke had up a head of steam, and he was still talking. "I can see a highwayman forcing his victim to dismount before shooting—gives him a chance to bring the horse under control first, if he plans to steal the horse. Known a lot who'd do it, too."

"But in that case—"

"In that case, the bullets would have struck at an angle. Exactly. So that's out."

Blacke scratched his head. "What I can't picture, out on the trail like that, is for the robber to dismount before shooting. No reason for it, and a lot of reasons not to. So he had to have shot him somewhere else."

While Blacke was talking, Doctor Mayhew had produced a basin and a brown bottle of carbolic, and was scrubbing his hands under a thin brown stream as his son poured. They then reversed the procedure.

When they were done, the doctor put the stopper back in the bottle and said, "Well, we have arrived at the same place by different destinations. It would be hard to hide that quantity of blood. Perhaps it should be looked for. However—"

"What's wrong with his hand?" I demanded.

"I was getting to that. You couldn't see it from your lower vantage point, Blacke, but the professor's right hand is rather badly burned."

"What? Let me see that." He wheeled his chair around the table and peered at the dead man's hand.

It was red and blistered against the whiteness of the skin between his index and middle finger, with some more burning along the base of the thumb and across the palm.

"What do you think happened, Doctor?" I asked. "Could he have been holding a cigar when he was shot and somehow not dropped it?"

The doctor shook his head. "No," he said. "Look."

From his pocket he took a small probe, a needle set in a wooden handle. Carefully, he pricked one of the blisters of the dead man's hand and pressed with the side of the needle. A clear fluid eased out.

"If you've ever had a blister yourself," the doctor said, "you'll be familiar with that fluid—basically blood serum. But the formation of blisters of that sort is a function of the healing process; it happens as the body attempts to ward off damage, or to repair itself after the damage has been done.

"In other words, blisters form only on a live body."

I felt suddenly ill.

"Do you mean he was tortured?"

"I don't know."

Now it was Blacke's turn to say no.

"He wasn't tortured," Blacke said. "Torturers like to be systematic, almost artistic. They wouldn't burn a man all in one place like that; not all on the same hand."

Blacke rubbed his own hand over his face. "No, Booker is right. The marks look like what would happen if a cigar burned down into his hand while he was holding it."

"Why would he do that?" I asked.

"Not saying he did. All I'm saying is that I'll bet the professor was holding something, or grabbed something that was red hot. And he did it shortly before he died."

"Must have hurt like fury," Merton said. We'd almost forgotten he was there.

Blacke looked wearily at him. "Not as bad as dying, boy," he said. "Not as bad as dying."

10

I SLEPT MOST of the next day, thanks to the laudanum, but the sleep was not peaceful, colored as it was by drug-amplified dreams of death and burning.

I was awake for several minutes before I could pry my eyelids apart. Almost as soon as I did, I heard a rapping on my door.

"Come in," I said. My voice was little better than a croak. I realized my throat was burning with thirst. I tried again, but sounded no better.

Rebecca came in with a pitcher of water and a tumbler on a tray. I noticed that she left the door open behind her as she approached the bed. She put the tray down on my bedside table, picked up the pitcher, and poured.

The water shimmered like diamonds. "Can you hold this?" she asked.

"I'll try," I rasped. After a night's rest, however troubled, my arms were working a lot better than my throat was. There was a soreness to them, but the insistent, in-the-bone ache of the night before had receded.

The water was ice cold, and I could feel it dissolving its way down my gullet. It was one of the most beautiful experiences of my life.

I drained the tumbler and handed it back to Rebecca.

"You are truly an angel of mercy," I said.

She smiled prettily. I had never noticed her dimples before.

"I heard you stirring, and I knew you'd be very thirsty. Louis needed laudanum quite a bit in the first days after his shooting, and he'd always awaken saying he felt as if his throat had been cut in the desert and sand poured in."

Apparently, I had been admitted to a new level of intimacy. She had said "Louis" rather than "my uncle." She was so lovely and kind and diplomatic, I knew it couldn't have been an accident. Someday I had to find out how such a young woman had fallen into her former life. That, however, was still a number of levels of intimacy away.

"That's a pretty good description," I said. "What time is it?"

"Past four o'clock. You slept for thirteen hours. You must be hungry."

"Not yet," I said, "but I will be by the time I get dressed."

"There's plenty left from last night—I mean this morning."

"I'm not surprised," I said.

Blacke and I had returned to the *Witness* building that morning to find a feast. Desperate with grief, Kate Sundberg had turned for diversion from it to the thing she knew best—cooking. At quarter past one in the morning, we sat down to a meal of ham, mashed potatoes, pancakes, scrambled eggs, biscuits, meatballs in brown gravy, and three dried-apple pies.

Tired and sore as I was, there was nothing to do but to sit down and eat it, which turned out to be a wise move. I had no idea how hungry I was until I had the first meatball in my mouth. Blacke and Rebecca tucked in, too. We had been going on nerves for hours; our bodies needed fuel. Mrs. Sundberg seemed to take some consolation from the fact that we ate so well. She said nothing, but poked in occasionally with another pitcher of cream for the pies, and favored us with a sad smile as we complimented her on the food.

But however hungrily we ate, ten of us could have worked at that food and not finished it. That, too, worked out for the best, since, Rebecca informed me, Mrs. Sundberg's fatigue had finally overtaken her grief, and she was now sleeping in her room.

Rebecca offered to bring me a tray of food.

"No, thanks," I said. "I want to test my legs. I also want to talk to Blacke."

"He's probably in his office. He's been there all day—he says he's working on his editorials for Wednesday's edition of the *Witness*."

"You say that as if you don't believe him."

"*I* think he's working on plans to catch the killer and avenge Mr. Sundberg's death."

"I think so, too. That's what I want to talk to him about."

"Mr. Booker—"

"Do you think by now you could force yourself to call me Quinn?"

"Quinn." She actually dropped her eyes and blushed when she said it. I'd heard of people turning over a new leaf, but Rebecca had turned over an entire forest.

She tried again and met my eyes this time. "Quinn, he's not a young man anymore, and he's confined to a wheelchair. He cannot go around seeking and confronting murderers. He's not a lawman anymore."

"He's still Lobo Blacke," I said. "He has the mind, and he has the soul, never mind the body. He didn't pick the newspaper business by accident, you know. He has a need to find the truth, and no number of bullets is going to stop him from trying unless they stop all of him—permanently."

"That's what I'm afraid of."

"Well, even if he didn't, I would. I was in that wagon, too. I have a few debts to pay."

"I worry about you, too." She took my hand and held it for a long moment. Her hand was soft and very warm.

"Don't worry too much," I said. "He's probably halfway to Denver by now."

"I don't think so," she said. "It's been snowing all day."

And that, I thought, puts paid to the idea of looking for cigar ashes or pools of blood, at least until springtime. I suppressed a sigh.

"Then maybe he's frozen to death out there somewhere. Not that it wouldn't serve him right, but I've never seen a hanging, and it strikes me he would be a good man to start with."

"If you insist on getting out of bed, I'll leave you to get dressed, then. I'll have some food ready for you."

"Thanks," I said.

"Mr. Booker. Quinn."

"Yes?"

"Watch out for him, won't you? And for yourself?"

"I promise."

Her amber eyes looked searchingly into mine for a moment. Then she started to laugh. "Men are such liars." It was the first time some of the brash old Becky had tinged the new demure Rebecca. She told me not to take too long, and left.

I threw the covers off and tried my luck at arising. It wasn't too bad. Like my arms, my legs and back were stiff and sore, but not the throbbing agonies they had been. I felt a lot less like a walking corpse and a lot more like tucking into some of that food.

I dressed and descended, sitting at the table just in time for Rebecca to deliver a trayful of cold ham and warm bread. I sliced them both, put meat between bread, spread mustard, and began to eat.

"I thought Mrs. Sundberg was sleeping."

"She is," Rebecca said. "She took a draft."

"This bread is fresh baked."

"Yes, it is. I baked it."

All I'd meant to say was that it was good bread, but my curse is that I try to be clever at inopportune times. What I said was, "There is no end to your talents, is there?"

Hearing this, she flushed, mumbled something about hoping I'd enjoy my meal, then left me cursing myself.

There was no sense lingering in the kitchen. I picked up my sandwich and a mug of cider and marched off to find Blacke.

He was, as predicted, in his office scowling at sheets of paper. These were not, however, foolscap on which he was writing editorials. They were diagrams and notes, scattered freely around a huge map of the area.

He spoke to me without looking up.

"Booker. About time you got here."

"Had you summoned me, I could have been here anytime."

"And have Becky riding me about hectoring an invalid? No, thank you. To hear her talking around here today, you'd never be able tell if the cripple around here was you or me."

He looked up as if trying to decide that for himself.

"You look better today than you did last night."

"I feel much better. Not all better, mind you. But much."

"I don't like food in here."

I stuffed the last of my sandwich into my mouth. "There," I said in a muffled voice. "It's gone."

"For an Eastern Gentleman, you can be awfully disgusting, Booker."

"I'm sorry," I said, washing down the sandwich with a swallow of cider. "I fled the kitchen after I accidentally hurt Rebecca's feelings."

"You what?"

I told him what I'd said and how she'd taken it.

"That's not like her. She has to know you didn't mean anything by it."

"Maybe she's upset about the murders."

Blacke rubbed his chin. "Maybe she is. But that's not like her, either. Not that she doesn't care—she's usually very levelheaded and tough."

"I hope there's no lingering resentment."

"Hell, if that happens, I'll get Doc Mayhew over here, snow and all."

"Oh, that reminds me." I got up and went to the window, hooked the curtain aside, and looked out. If it had indeed been snowing all day, it had been snowing slowly. The town was covered with white, but not to any great depth. Enough to ruin a search for the missing items, but not enough to keep the killer from getting away.

"Look at the map, Booker," Blacke commanded.

I looked.

"I've marked the places where the attacks were made. The S stands for where you and Sundberg were attacked; the P for where you found the professor."

"All right."

"Anything strike you as odd about this?"

"Well, to judge by the map, Vessemer was at the edge of town when he was struck down. It didn't seem that close to me."

"City limits. The built-up area is some way further on. But the point is, did you ever know a highwayman to operate that close to a town?"

"I'm from New York City. All the bad men I know operate right in the middle of town."

"Not on horseback. Not against another man on horseback who can flee and summon armed help after a chase of less than a minute."

"You mean the killer was someone the professor knew?"

"It's possible."

"I didn't recognize him."

"You've been here less than a week; the professor's visited Le Four at this season for years. And, Booker, you were running for your life, then jumping for it. You were hardly in a position to recognize your *own* face, let alone a killer's. Besides, he was masked, wasn't he?"

"Yes. He was. I wonder if I *would* have recognized him if I'd seen him."

Blacke shook his head. "That's not the question."

"What is?"

"Why you're alive."

"I assume you don't mean that in the metaphysical sense."

Blacke snorted. "I couldn't if I wanted to, since I don't know what the hell that word means."

"It means—"

"Tell me later. I want to talk this out with you. It's not so much that we don't know anything, it's that what we do know makes no sense."

"Go ahead."

Blacke picked up a scrap of paper. "All right. First the attack on you and Sundberg. He wanted to stop you, but he didn't want to kill you. In fact, he was planning not to kill you. Killing Sundberg was just bad luck."

"Especially for Sundberg," I said.

"Dammit, Booker," Blacke snapped. "The man's widow is under this roof. Jokes are out of place."

"I was being bitter," I said.

"I don't think Mrs. Sundberg, if she overheard you, would be in the mood to tell the difference, do you?"

I conceded that he had a point.

"But why do you say he didn't want to kill us?" I demanded. "He certainly didn't wish us well."

"I say it because he was masked. If he was planning to kill you, the mask was unnecessary. Worse, it made his job harder, especially if it was someone you would recognize. He could use that familiarity to draw up level with you, pull a gun, and kill you at his convenience. Even if it was a stranger to you, a masked man is a lot more suspicious than one with a naked face."

"I see. So he wore the mask because he knew we'd be around after the attack—or he thought we would—and he didn't want us to be able to recognize him." I shut up and thought for a second. "That means it was someone who was planning to stay around town."

"It makes sense that way," Blacke said. "Now. *Why* didn't he kill you?"

"I don't know." It's a horrible feeling not to know why someone didn't murder you, if only because of the unsettling awareness that he might soon change his mind.

"I do."

"Yes?"

"At least I think I do. I may be wrong."

"Tell me."

"It's the only way that makes sense, as far as I can see. . . ."

"Tell me!"

The gray eyes looked at me innocently. "I'm going to, I'm going to. Keep your shirt on."

"You enjoy this, don't you?"

He scowled and said I must be crazy, but I could see the excited gleam in his eye. If he couldn't chase the outlaws on the trail, at least he could match wits with them here.

"He wanted you alive because he wanted you to find the professor's body."

"If he'd just let us keep riding, we would have found it."

"Maybe not," Blacke said. "Remember, the professor was killed somewhere else and *brought* out to the trail just outside of town. Does that suggest anything to you?"

"That he was killed *in* town?" It was something I hadn't thought of before.

"Exactly," Blacke said. "Waylaid on the trail, brought somewhere at gunpoint, killed, and brought back to the trail just outside of town and dumped."

"That leaves us with the question of why he did *that*. Or do you think you have the answer to that one, too?"

"As a matter of fact . . ."

"All right, give," I demanded.

"Why don't you see if you can work it out for yourself."

I was going to point out that he'd probably spent the day working on this, while I had spent it in a drugged stupor, but he probably would have made some remark about it, so I let it go. Instead, I concentrated on the challenge itself.

"Very well. Let's see, what did he gain by wrecking me? He gained time to catch up with the professor, get to town with him, kill him, and dump him back on the trail."

"So far, so good."

"So why did he need to bring the professor to town to kill him? He didn't. So he must have brought the professor to town for something else. Something the professor could do that the killer couldn't.

"What was that?" I wondered. "In town . . ."

I hit my fist on Blacke's desk. "The Pullman car. The professor's Pullman car with all his photographic files. If the killer didn't want to be recognized—"

"You're there, son. That's the way it shapes up to me. So you know what I'd do, now, if I was my old self?"

"You'd find a way to get inside the car to see what's missing."

"I sure would, especially in this town. Ordinarily, that'd be the sheriff's job, but brother Harlan couldn't be trusted to spill piss from a boot if the instructions were written on the heel."

"You could trust him to steal the boot," I offered.

Blacke grinned. "Only if it wasn't Jenkins's boot."

"True," I said. "I did get the impression he knew not to offend the Great God Jenkins."

"God is right. But forget about that. The point is, what do we do about the Pullman car?"

"Seems obvious to me, boss. I go out there and take a look around."

"Are you up to it?"

"I'm touched by your concern," I began.

"Don't mock me, Booker."

"I wouldn't dream of it. I really am touched by your concern. Granted, I am not your old self. At this point, I am not even *my* old self. But whether he wanted me dead or not, there's someone out there who put my life in danger and killed two men I had respect and regard for. I can walk, and I can see, and I can force a lock with the right tool, and I'm going over there."

"You're sure?"

"I'm positive. Having come to the conclusions we've come to, I wouldn't be comfortable without checking them in any case. If I overdo it, I can take more laudanum and sleep away tomorrow."

Blacke made a face. "Be careful with that stuff. The more you take the more you need. You can get to the point where you're better off with the pain."

"I'll be careful."

"Dress up warm. Sneak out when Becky can't see you, or she'll make a goddam fuss."

"You sound like my grandmother. Except for the cursing, of course.

"One more thing," I said.

"Yes?"

"I want a gun."

"I was about to suggest that very thing." Blacke reached to his desk and opened a drawer.

11

THE WALK DOWN Main Street from the *Witness* office to the railroad station wasn't too bad. The snow wasn't so much flakes as a fine, gritty powder, like the sand in an hourglass, perhaps even finer. Blown by the wind, it scoured the face, but it was easy enough to walk in.

As I pressed on with my head bent forward and my gloved hands in my pockets, my right hand was sharing space with a small, nickel-plated revolver given me by Blacke.

I had asked for a proper gun, but Blacke pointed out that that would require a holster, which in turn would require my unbuttoning my greatcoat to get at the gun if I needed to use it.

I wasn't entirely convinced, but I let it go, because during the walk something else occurred to me—proof positive that Vessemer had been back to his studio last night.

The cigar case we'd seen at Doctor Mayhew's office had been full, yet that was an impossibility. I had seen him smoking several cigars last night (it was hard to believe it was only last night) at Martha Jenkins's party. I had seen him take at least one from the cigar case. Therefore, it could not be full unless he had managed to refill it, and he could have done that nowhere but at his private car.

Involuntarily, I quickened my steps.

It was a good thing I did. The professor's car was across the way, on a siding on the south side of the railway yard. I had it in my sights, and I was heading for it. I had a story ready (or a few dollars if necessary) to deal with the guard, but I didn't see him and he didn't approach me, something I chalked up to Sunday-evening languor.

I was about thirty yards away when I saw the smoke. It rose up from a point almost precisely in the middle of the car. Ignoring angry muscles, I stooped to look under the bottom of the car to see if I could detect any flames.

I saw no flames, but I did see legs scurrying rapidly away. I ran, clumsily and painfully, to the Pullman and around it, but by the time I got there, the fugitive was out of sight. I knew I had no chance of catching him even if I had been in peak condition, so I turned my attention to the professor's car.

Now I saw flames. Someone had doused the door of the railway car with kerosene and set it alight. The bright green paint had begun to blister and peel and the flames had just begun to bite and char the wood.

I stood there stupidly for a moment, then began to fight the blaze. I threw a double handful of snow at the flames, and it helped, where it reached. The problem was it didn't cover a wide enough area of the burning wood. A couple more handfuls made me realize that the flames could spread faster than I could douse them, at least this way.

I took off my greatcoat and spread it on the ground, then proceeded to pile snow on it.

"*What* do you think you're doing?" asked an imperious voice. A woman's voice. I looked up to see Abigail Jenkins glaring at me. The glare faded to surprise as she saw my face.

"Trying to put out this fire," I said. I bent again and piled more snow.

She ran toward me, leaving little prints in the snow. "I thought you were horribly injured."

"Horrible is a relative term," I said.

"But why are you—"

"Explanations can wait. Why don't you shut up, make yourself useful, and help me?"

A look of combined shock and anger passed over her face. The daughter of Lucius Jenkins was not used to being spoken to in this manner, and she was going to tell me so. Then a curious look came into her dark eyes. Without a word, she discarded her fur muff and, barehanded, began to scoop snow with me.

In a few moments, we had a respectable pile on the coat. I doubled up the cloth, picked it up, ran to the burning portion of the car, and then flung the coat open, bringing a veritable avalanche to bear on the flames. For good measure, I held the coat against the charred area to smother any embers.

It wasn't until after I had done this that I remembered the loaded revolver in the pocket. Fortunately, whatever heat there was was insufficient to cause the bullets to fire. Shooting myself that way would have been embarrassing; shooting Abigail Jenkins would have been disastrous.

I took the coat away and looked at it. It was a sooty mess, but not severely damaged. I was cold. I put it back on, then retrieved Abigail's muff. Before giving it to her, I removed my gloves and chafed her frozen hands in mine. When they were not so icy to the touch, I handed her the muff and said, "Thank you for your help. I don't think I could have done it without you."

"You are quite welcome," she said. "Now, about those explanations."

"What would you like to know?"

"Who set this fire? What are you doing here? What are you doing up at all? To hear the sheriff tell it, he only let you out of custody out of Christian charity, because you were at death's door and needed medical attention."

"To take your questions in order," I said. "The fire was set by the person who made those footprints." Even as I pointed to them, they were disappearing, filled with windblown snow. "I can't identify him any further, unfortunately. I came here because Blacke and I have come to the conclusion that there is something worth learning in Vessemer's Pullman. We know that it's the sheriff's job to do this, but frankly, I don't think he's up to it. I pause to let you comment."

"Oh," she said airily. "I suspect we have similar opinions on a number of things. Do go on."

" The reason I'm up at all is that my injuries are inconvenient, rather than dire, and I decided that peace of mind was worth a certain amount of pain."

"I *knew* we'd agree on a lot of things. Shall we go inside? Are you going to shoot off the lock?"

"No, I am not going to shoot off the lock. And before *we* do anything, why don't you answer a couple of questions for me?"

She nodded. "It seems only fair," she said gravely.

I cupped her chin in my hand. Her black eyes grew wide.

"Miss Jenkins," I said.

"Call me Abigail."

"Not yet. Miss Jenkins, you interest me strangely; it may turn out that we are to be friends."

"I hope so."

"But there is something you should know about me. I cannot abide being mocked by a woman."

"Oh. Then I won't do it anymore."

I continued to stare at her.

"I promise," she said.

"Good." I took my hand away—I had left a smudge on the corner of her chin. I decided to tell her about it later. Or not, depending on how well she kept her promise.

"Now," I said, "what are *you* doing here?"

"Oh, Father and Mother and Sir Peter and I and a few of the servants came in to give statements to the sheriff about what happened last night at the party, if we'd noticed anything suspicious."

"Did you?"

"Of course not. Did you?"

"Not until it was too late."

She nodded. "There you are, then. The whole trip was a waste of time. I am personally of the opinion that Father wanted to talk to the sheriff not to answer questions but to tell the fool what to do. The rest of us were dragged along to make it look good."

"Whom does your father think he's fooling?" I asked. "I've been here less than a week, but I already know he runs the town."

"I know. It's really quite tiresome. As was the session with the sheriff. They took me first, thank goodness, and I left to take a walk. I found myself down this end of town, and I saw the smoke, so I looked into it, and found you."

"But you didn't find the guard. And he didn't find you."

"No sign of him."

I considered looking for the man. If I were going to commit a little arson, I'd want to make sure the guard was out of the way first; he might be hurt.

Of course, the guard might also be dead, and I lacked the will to put myself in a position of finding another dead body. The sheriff would probably lock me up again.

Furthermore, what I was about to do was completely illegal, and if the guard was simply having an early-Sunday-evening nap, my waking him would only ruin my plans.

The next thing to decide was what to do with Abigail. I decided to keep her along. She knew too much already to make the effort of shooing her worthwhile. If she could be shooed.

And, practically speaking, if we got caught rifling a dead man's quarters, the fact that I was doing it in company with Lucius Jenkins's daughter would go a long way toward getting me off the hook.

I walked to the door of the Pullman, removed a glove, and held my hand close. No heat came to me; the door was probably cool enough to touch.

So far so good. I had told Abigail that I wasn't going to shoot the lock, which was fine. The question was, what *was* I going to do? I had a small iron bar in the back of my belt that I could pry the door open with. That might have been quieter than a bullet, but still cumbersome and messy. You'd think that Lobo Blacke, with all his vast acquaintance of the scum of the West, could have added someone to his staff who was skilled at picking locks.

I grabbed the handle and gave a pull. I learned that the putative scum in question would not have been needed in the case. The door was open. I remembered that there were no keys among the professor's belongings.

I flipped down the stairs to the car and pulled the little revolver from my pocket.

"Goodness," Abigail said.

"Just a precaution," I told her.

I went up and stepped inside. I had been half expecting bedlam, a cyclone of smashed furniture and scattered photographs, but I found nothing of the sort. A lantern still burned dimly in the car; a large wooden camera lay on a tripod. The professor's large filing cabinets were neatly pushed in. A half-glass of wine remained undrunk on a small table.

There were only two untidy things in the whole room.

The first was a gray envelope about ten inches square that sat on the same table as the glass of wine. PHOTOGRAPHIC PRINT FOR QUINN BOOKER had been written on it.

As I picked up the envelope, I heard the rustle of skirts and petticoats behind me.

"Don't touch anything," I said.

"You're touching something," she pointed out.

"It's addressed to me."

Her voice was scornful. "That doesn't make any difference. We're not supposed to be in here."

Even more irritating than a mocking woman is a woman who is *right*.

"As a personal favor," I said, trying not to grit my teeth, "indulge me by touching nothing, please?"

"Since you put it so nicely." She looked around the car. "I've always liked this place. Liked coming here much better than actually sitting for a photograph. But Mother will have our beauty recorded."

"She'll have to find some other means to do it, now."

"So she will," Abigail mused. "Or take up photography herself. That's a gruesome thought. I shall miss Professor Vessemer. What's in the envelope that bothers you so?"

I tried to ease the scowl on my face, but I probably didn't succeed. What bothered me so much was that there was *nothing* in the envelope. I had been expecting, of course, the photograph of myself holding young Marvin at bay.

I opened a few drawers of the filing system. I checked under my name and Marvin's, but nothing was there for either of us. A look under "Jenkins" produced a fat file. I looked through it briefly. I learned that Abigail had been beautiful even as a child, but I learned little else.

I sighed. It was time to face the other thing wrong in the room. On the carpeting at the far end of the car, as if gathering itself to pose for a photograph, was a large pool of brownish, gelid blood.

We had found the murder scene.

12

MONDAY AFTERNOON, LUCIUS Jenkins dropped in. Blacke reached for the checkerboard; Jenkins doffed his coat but (as usual) kept his hat on as he sat down.

As they set up the board, Jenkins said, "How are you feeling, Booker?"

"Just a second," I said. I was setting my story of the fire and the discovery of the pool of blood in type for Wednesday's paper. With Sundberg, our resident swift, dead, we had to do these things in advance. Merton Mayhew came by after school to help; he had a flair for it, skillful hands like a surgeon.

I was all right—I had pitched in sometimes back east—but something about my brain made me incapable of reading smoothly upside down and backwards, a vital skill for a truly excellent typesetter.

I finished a paragraph, put down the composing stick, and said, "Sorry, Mr. Jenkins. I have to concentrate when I'm doing that. I'm fine. A little stiff, but recovering."

"Good, good." He turned his eyes from me to the checkerboard. Blacke was feigning indifference, but he knew his old friend was working up to saying something.

"Feel up to sitting a horse?" Jenkins asked. "You do ride, don't you?"

"I do. I think I could manage it, with the proper incentive."

"Well, that's for you to judge. Asa Harlan and a few deputies are riding out to my spread to arrest that fool Marvin. Since you're at least partly responsible, I thought you might want to ride along and write it up all nice for Blacke's paper."

"How is he responsible?" Blacke asked blandly.

"Why, Louis, he had that picture taken, humiliating the boy. He killed the professor to get it back."

"That's the most ridic—"

Blacke cut me off. "Interesting theory, Lucius. What happens now?"

"Asa arrests Marvin." The bald man shrugged. "He'll hang, I suppose."

"Then Marvin's brother comes gunning for Booker."

Jenkins grinned. "I'm sure the sheriff will stop that from happening."

"The sheriff," Blacke said, "couldn't stop a bunghole with a cork. *You* will keep it from happening, Lucius, for two reasons. One, if anything happens, I will fill every paper west of St. Louis and a lot of the eastern ones, too, with stories about how you used to keep this town peaceable by putting all the thugs on your payroll, but how things are getting out of control."

"You've known me a long time, Louis. Did I ever strike you as a man who cares a whole lot about what other people think?"

"No," Blacke said flatly. "But your wife cares. Cares a great deal, doesn't she? Dreams of somehow getting Abigail back east and into Society. I can fix that."

If Blacke could prevent Abigail from ever becoming a part of eastern Society, my personal opinion would be that he was doing her a favor. But I held my tongue.

Jenkins grunted and moved a checker. "What's your other reason?"

"Spring's coming. Roundup. Branding. You're going to need all the hands you can get, even if they are bullies and hoorahs."

"I don't follow you."

"You're already losing Marvin. Don't lose Frank, too."

"You mean, he'll be arrested?" Jenkins's face showed how little he believed that.

"I mean that if he comes causing trouble, Booker will kill him."

Jenkins laughed. I'd be laughing, too, except I was too busy being furious with Blacke. He might as well have painted a target on my back. I killed a deer up near Bear Mountain once; that was the extent of my lethal tendencies. Good eating, but nothing like killing a man.

Deep down, I wasn't sure I could if I had to.

Jenkins turned to me.

"What do you say to that, Booker?"

I had two choices—to brazen it out, or to make both my employer and myself look like complete fools.

"I don't like to swagger," I said.

"But . . . ," Jenkins urged.

"But nothing. I don't like to, so I won't do it. I'll just say one thing. If you think Le Four is tough, you've never walked through Five Points on a Saturday night. A lot of things have to happen before Mr. Blacke's assertion is tested. I hope they never do. But if they do, and if Frank is determined to find out, he will find out. I'll find out. We'll all find out."

We sure will, I thought. I just hoped we'd like the results.

Time to change the subject. "When is the sheriff going?" I asked.

"They planned to leave at two."

I looked at the clock. "Gives me just enough time to get ready," I said. I tied up the type and placed it in a galley, used some spirits to clean my hands, took off my apron, adjusted my tie, and reached in a drawer for a gunbelt. It was black with age and supple, though it hadn't been worn for years. It clung to my waist like a lover's arms, and the weight of the unfancy, unnotched .45 pressed my right hip as if it belonged there.

This was the gun of Lobo Blacke, and there had been a time when putting it on would have been an honor and a thrill; now it was a burden. It wasn't that I'd lost any of my admiration for Lobo Blacke—I had simply gained an appreciation of the power of a gun.

Merton had volunteered to saddle one of the horses for me, this one a chestnut mare with a black mane and tail, called Posy. She was waiting around the front. I was climbing into the saddle when the sheriff rode by with his men.

It wasn't a big posse—four men. I knew a couple of them, Walker, the greengrocer, and Steinmetz, the ironmonger.

"Afternoon," the sheriff said.

"Same to you, Sheriff. Gentlemen." We touched hat brims all around.

"Raise your right hand," Asa Harlan said.

"What for?"

"The oath. You don't get your badge without you take the legal oath."

"I don't want a badge."

"Dammit, if you're in the posse, you got to have a badge."

"Ah. I think I see what the problem is. I'm not in the posse, Mr. Harlan." I said it slowly and calmly, as though explaining to a recalcitrant child, a description not all that removed from the truth.

"You ain't in the posse," the sheriff said.

"No."

"Then why the blazes are you coming along, then?"

"I'm coming as a journalist," I explained. "You've complained about how we write about you in the *Witness* in the past, haven't you?"

"Who wouldn't?"

"Well, I'm still new in town; I've written nothing about you. I want to be completely fair. I want my observations to be fresh. I want to see with my own eyes the way you handle your job. I want to forget that unfortunate misunderstanding we had the other night."

"You didn't write about that yet?"

"There may be no need to. We may have bigger stories to tell than that."

"You might? Hah! I'll see that you do. Keep your eyes open and your pen ready, Mr. Booker. Men, let's ride!"

He actually pointed his finger down Main Street to show them the way. He was indisputably sitting taller in the saddle. In his mind he had to be at least Ulysses S. Grant on the way to Appomattox; possibly Washington crossing the Delaware.

I was so impressed, I pulled out my pocketbook and pencil and pretended to make a note.

For a good half hour, Harlan's notion of leadership included stern silence, which suited me fine. I could devote the moments to plotting revenge on Blacke for putting me on the spot with Frank. Just thinking about it made the gun uncomfortable on my hip.

I could also contemplate the ridiculousness of the fool's errand I was curiously on.

Marvin hadn't killed Sundberg and the professor. The very thought was absurd. Not that I didn't believe Marvin would never kill anybody; he'd tried to kill *me*.

The point was that Marvin didn't have enough imagination to conceive killing someone and moving the body to gain time for a search of some premises. Marvin wouldn't even think of *searching* anybody's premises. He'd just torch the whole thing and trust to luck that the picture had been destroyed.

And speaking of torching things, it was a known fact that Marvin hadn't been the one trying to burn down the Pullman on Sunday afternoon. A circuit-riding preacher called Brother Ambrose had hit the Jenkins spread, and Marvin, along with half the hands and most of the house staff, had been out there all Sunday afternoon listening to him paint word pictures of the horrors of hell and the glories of heaven.

The sheriff's theory, from what Jenkins had let slip to Blacke while I was getting my coat and gloves on, was that the fire at the Pullman car had been the work of some vandal. Marvin had done the murder Saturday night because he didn't trust us not to show the picture to Abigail. He'd waylaid the professor, brought him to the railroad car, made him find the photograph, then shot him in the back like the coward everybody knew he was.

Of course, that *didn't* explain why the so-called random vandal had bothered to carefully knock out and tie up the railroad guard (Abigail and I found him asleep peacefully on the floor of his shed) in order to set fire to that particular car.

An especially inefficient fire, too. Lit at the place on the car where the most metal was, where the smoke was most likely to be seen the earliest.

Blacke and I had talked it over yesterday evening. I'd walked into the *Witness* office and taken off my hat and coat.

"You've been gone a long time. What did you find?"

I told him.

"Why didn't you boot her tail out of there?" he demanded.

"How well do you know her?"

He chuckled. "You've got me there. I know her well enough to doubt she's bootable."

"Besides, she *did* help me put the fire out."

"So naturally, you had to go do your duty as a citizen and tell Harlan all about it."

"I could hardly skip it with Abigail Jenkins having seen what she'd seen. I could have sworn her to secrecy, but why should I think she'd stick to it?"

"You should have kissed her a good one."

I looked at him. "You're unbelievable," I said. "It so happens that in the presence of a pool of coagulating gore on the carpet, neither of us was in the mood."

"All right, all right."

"Not that the idea of kissing the young woman is at all repugnant."

"There's better women around," Blacke asserted. "Prettier. Sweeter. Just gotta keep your eyes open."

I was silent for a few moments, trying to decide what he was talking about. Then I got an idea about it that so startled me, I had to get back the point immediately.

In the event, though, I didn't have to. Blacke did it for me.

"But forget all that," he said. "What do you make of what happened today?"

"I think," I said, "I took somebody's bait."

He nodded approvingly. "You're starting to think like a lawman. Go on."

"That fire wasn't meant to destroy anything. It was deliberately set up to be smoky and nondestructive in order to draw attention to the professor's private car."

"Who would do that? And why?"

"Are you trying to tell me you really can't guess?"

"No. I'm trying to see if your ideas mesh with mine. It's not too much trouble, is it? I mean, I am paying you a salary."

With some people, sarcasm is a blade. With Lobo Blacke, it's a bludgeon. To avoid further bruising, I went on.

"The killer would do that. He'd do it to get someone to search the car."

"And establish the real place of death? I thought he moved the body to disguise it."

"To gain time for his search. But he was done with it by Sunday. Probably done with it a lot sooner, and he was getting impatient with the sheriff and with us for not searching the thing."

"Why did he want the search made?"

"Oh," I said. "That's an easy one. He wanted somebody to find the envelope addressed to me."

"Mmmm," Blacke said. "Awfully convenient, that envelope being right out on a table like that, wasn't it?"

"It was indeed. You might as well have hung a sign outside saying, '*Hey, that picture's missing, arrest Marvin.*'"

"So you think somebody's trying to frame Marvin?"

"I think somebody *has* framed Marvin. It's just a matter of the sheriff's stupidity and Jenkins's willingness to shield the boy that will decide whether he gets arrested or not. Either way, I expect it will end the search—the official one, anyway—and suit the killer fine."

"I'll tell you something else that will suit the killer fine."

"What's that?"

"Well, with the professor dead, and his assistant laid up back in Minneapolis, we have no idea exactly what was in the professor's files to start with, do we?"

I got what he was driving at. "So we don't know *what else* might have been taken."

Looked at in the proper light, that whole conversation was a lesson in futility. We may have used up enough brainpower to enlighten the entire West; we may have used the scalpel of logic to cut healthy Truth from the rotting corpse of Error; we might have done any wonderful mental thing you could imagine.

Yet here I was, riding with a posse headed by a man I despised, on the way to arrest someone I was sure was innocent, with the almost certain result of my becoming a target of murderous revenge by the innocent man's brother.

13

OF COURSE, THOUGHTS like those point the road to madness. I decided to concentrate on not making a fool of myself in front of the posse.

You see, as I told Jenkins, I did ride. Had been riding from childhood, in fact. But I had learned to ride eastern style. In the East, we don't do a lot of roping due to a lack of ropeworthy animals. Therefore, we use a different saddle, one that is smaller, thinner, and virtually pommelless.

We also post. Posting is a kind of jumping in the stirrups. When the horse goes down, we go up. It's supposed to keep our heads level, or something.

In any case, four years ago, in Boulder, my first trip west, I had made myself a source of real amusement to the cowboys and other westerners who saw me for the first time on horseback, bouncing up and down in the huge armchair of a western saddle.

It was Blacke (who had had Rebecca wheel him to the window to see what all the ruckus was about) who had told me what was so funny and had given me the advice to cure it: "Sit on the damned animal like you enjoy being there."

I caught on pretty well, but there was always the temptation to forget and backslide. For all sorts of reasons, I would rather be rubbed with sand and then splashed with carbolic before I gave Asa Harlan an excuse to laugh at me. I concentrated on keeping my hindquarters where they belonged.

We took a side trail off the main road and so escaped sight of Bellevue altogether. Instead, we soon came to a low, gray, one-story structure that actually looked like a ranch. This was where Stick Witherspoon, the ranch foreman, lived, and where the hands bunked. We were probably two or three miles from Mrs. Jenkins's palace, but we might as well have been on another continent.

Witherspoon walked out to greet us. He had the look of a slim man who late in life had latched on to a sort of cooking that he really liked, because he had a little round ball of a belly just above his belt.

He was coatless. It was warmer than it had been, but it wasn't *that* warm. The sun was bright and had burned away a lot of yesterday's powdery snow, the way it does, but it was still cold.

"How can I help you, Sheriff?"

"I'm here for Marvin Hastings. Seems he killed the professor."

"Marvin?" Witherspoon almost squeaked. "He can't ride well enough to have caught up with the professor, let alone killed him."

Hmmm, I thought. There was a reason that hadn't occurred to Blacke or me.

The sheriff wasn't having any. "He done it, right enough. Now, where is he?"

"He's not here. He rode down to the south range with some of the real punchers. Never done that before. Maybe you're right at that, Sheriff."

"Why don't you come along and show us the way?" suggested Steinmetz.

The sheriff shot a glance at me, then an angry glare at Steinmetz. I knew what he was thinking. If Witherspoon showed the way, it might be thought he was *leading* the posse, and that glory was to go only to Sheriff Asa Harlan.

I wasn't worried about glory; I only wanted to get this over with. I said to the sheriff, "Smart move. The more men in your command, the greater general you are."

"Okay, Stick, don't take all day, if you're coming," Harlan said gruffly. He reacted in a magisterial way when Witherspoon suggested they water their horses while he saddled up.

I dismounted and walked around. I went over and introduced myself to Witherspoon.

"I know who you are," he said. His tone was neither friendly nor unfriendly. "You're that dude from back east who can walk on water."

"There's a lot of things I can do," I said. "Have you noticed Marvin's behavior over the last couple of days?"

"What do you mean?"

"Has he been acting any differently?"

"No, he's been his usual obnoxious self. Him and those friends of his."

"Where are those friends of his, come to think of it?" It had occurred to me that it might be a good idea to get in the habit of keeping track of where Frank and his cronies were whenever we were in the same general vicinity.

"I got them round the back, breaking ice off the well." He grinned. "Mr. Jenkins went to town without them. Second time in a row, and they don't like it."

"Not used to actual work, are they?"

"No, they are not. It's Mr. Jenkins's money, he can hire bodyguards, strong-arm men, or anything else he likes to call them, but why he sticks them in the bunk with the real punchers is too much for me."

"Are you sure they're still digging in the well?"

"They were when I heard you fellers ride up."

"I want to ask you a little more about Marvin."

"Oh, *why*, for God's sake?" He pulled a buckle tight, checked it, then went around the horse and did another.

"I ask myself the same question. I guess it's because while it's the posse's job to get him, it's my job to get the truth."

"Good luck on that one. Look, mister, I'm about ready, here."

"Just a question or two more. I only met Marvin twice, but does he strike you as the type who could kill a man, and just go on being his usual obnoxious self?"

"Now that you mention it, no. I s'pose that's another reason I think the sheriff is blowin' wind about him doing it."

"Seems to me," I went on, "that if Marvin killed somebody, he'd either be bragging about it, or cringing in fear. Maybe both, at two-hour intervals."

"You're right, at that. I got no use for the little toad, but you're right about that. Although he was acting a little nervous this morning, just before Mr. Jenkins left for town."

I nodded. "Nervous enough to ask for work."

"Yeah." Stick laughed. "Maybe he was afraid of what I'd have him doing if he let *me* think of something." He got suddenly serious. "But I'd bet my left leg he didn't kill those people, and from what you say, you're thinking that way, too."

"I am."

"You got any ideas on what to do about it?"

"Only one. Ride with the sheriff and let him know he's being watched. Marvin's a lot less likely to come back dead that way."

He squinted at me. "Looks like you got a pretty good fix on our sheriff on brief acquaintance, too, haven't you?"

"It's a gift," I told him.

The sheriff's voice came from outside. "You two comin'? I got a killer to catch. Like to do it before dark."

"Be right there," Stick told him. To me, in an undertone, he said, "If he don't find him before dark, he'll never find his way back home."

With Stick duly deputized (he wasn't thrilled with the idea, but he didn't have the excuse I had) the posse formed up and rode south, where the flat land suddenly broke out in a mild case of rocks and hills. Quite rugged, in a minor way, and surprising, because we came up on it so suddenly. Past here, according to Stick, was the south range, where we ought to find young Marvin Hastings.

The sheriff and a couple members of his posse checked their guns, which I supposed was prudent.

It turned out to be downright sagacious.

We were riding a passage through a couple of rocks, single file, although there was room for a couple of horses to go abreast if need be. The sheriff was talking about how when statehood came, he was going to stop all this manhunting and go into politics, where his talents would really be appreciated.

"With all the fighting I've done for people right here, Booker, I could really fight for them in Washington as a governor or a senator."

My horse was directly behind his, third in line, with Stick in the lead. Stick took the first bullet.

The shot rang out, sharp and high as it echoed off the rocks. Stick grabbed his thigh and fell from the horse.

The echoes hadn't died away when more shots came. They didn't do any damage that I could see, but they did cause confusion, with horses rearing and shying at the noise.

It was obvious that the shots were coming from above. I figured my best chance was to dismount and hug the rock wall, which I did as soon as my horse deigned to put four feet on the ground at once. I found a little niche in the wall and drew my gun. Lobo Blacke's gun. The four riders behind me when the shooting started had managed to get turned around and had gone back out the other way.

Sheriff Asa Harlan was still on horseback, peering up at the rocks, daring the cowardly bushwhacker to show himself. No brains, I thought, but plenty of guts.

Meanwhile, Stick Witherspoon was lying in the middle of everything, as exposed as an egg sunny-side up. He was trying to crawl but afraid to let go of his leg.

"Sheriff!" I yelled.

"What?" he demanded. He turned to look at me, and immediately another shot came down, making the sheriff's horse rear violently. Harlan was thrown and hit the rocks hard, but he bounced up like a round-bottomed doll, cursing and shooting.

"Don't look at me," I said, as I probably should have at first. "Just keep firing. Keep the shooter's head down. I'm going to get Stick to safety."

"Yeah?" He sounded surprised. "All right, Booker, you got it."

Harlan started a barrage at where the shooter ought to be. I dashed out from the rocks, myself, squeezing off a few shots to let the sheriff reload. Then I grabbed Stick by the collar and dragged him unceremoniously back to my little niche in the wall.

Before I got there, though, I got a split-second peek at the face peering over the top of the rock. Marvin. The sight of me seemed to make him go wild. He screamed unflattering remarks about my ancestry, and was loud but incoherent on the subject of the photograph.

He raised his gun as if determined to get me, but by that time, the sheriff's piece was back in action, and he had to duck again or get his head blown off.

Once under cover, I took a look at Stick's leg. He was right not to let go of it. It was a bad one, possibly an artery. I pulled open his sheepskin coat to get at the grimy blue bandanna I'd seen around his neck. I held it by diagonally opposite corners and rolled it up tight.

"Hurry up with that, will ya?" Stick gasped.

"I'm going as quickly as I can. Just keep squeezing."

I whipped the rolled-up bandanna around his thigh above the wound and tied a tight knot. Now I needed something to twist in it. I could have used the barrel of the gun I'd put back in the holster, but I was loath to ~~give~~ it up in the current circumstances. Also, with my luck, I'd be ~~catching~~ the thing in the fabric, and it would go off and blow Stick's chin away. It only occurs to me now as I write this that I could have unloaded the gun.

No matter. I remembered something to use. It involved delving through layers of clothing, but I unearthed it in a few seconds. It was a pen, solid silver, bought to celebrate the printing of the tenth thousand of *The Memoirs of Lobo Blacke*. My most prized possession; I generally used it to sign checks.

I pushed it through between bandanna and thigh and twisted. The pen was stout and strong and worked perfectly. As I tightened the tourniquet, I could see the seepage of blood from under Stick's fingers lessen and finally stop.

"Let go," I said.

"Are you sure?" The words were wrung out of him past the pain. They hardly sounded human.

"I'm sure. If I'm wrong, we can grab it again."

Stick took his hands away. The wound was a raw, ugly mess, and the leg of his pants was sodden with blood, but no blood gushed from the hole.

While all this was going on, something else had happened, or rather, had ceased to happen. There were no more gunshots.

"Sheriff?" I called.

"Yeah. I think the other four flushed him. I hope they shot the bastard. No I don't, I hope they left him for me."

He got his wish. I told Stick to stay put, I'd round up a horse to put him on. I stood up—gun ready—and went to join the sheriff. He said he'd help me in the roundup. We walked to the end of the defile, and out on the flat ground again, we saw Marvin being chased by three other riders. The sheriff's horse, a well-trained beast, was waiting for him. He said, "Hot damn," pulled a rifle out of a saddle scabbard, clambered up some rocks, took aim at the lead figure, and fired twice.

Now I knew what else, besides raw foolhardy courage, Asa Harlan was good for. He could shoot.

So far out as to be a dot in the distance, Marvin fell from his horse, rolled, and lay still.

Now, I'm a pretty good shot, rifle and pistol. Colonel Bogardus Booker made sure of that with strappings if I missed the bull. But I had *never* seen shooting like that.

"Hot damn!" the sheriff said again. "I'll be back with a horse," he said. He mounted up and headed out for the horizon. I had a look around but couldn't find any horses within reach. I called Posy's name a few times, but the beast didn't know me well enough to come.

I went back to Stick. Mercifully, he was unconscious. I loosened the tourniquet for a minute or so, not enough to let blood gush, but enough to let it flow so that the leg wouldn't turn black and die on him.

The sheriff and his posse returned before my watch said I had to loosen the tourniquet again. Harlan had Marvin draped over Marvin's own horse like a hunter returning with meat for the pot. He also had Posy and Stick's horse with him.

The next stop was back at the ranch house, where we picked up a buckboard to carry the wounded to the doctor and the dead to the undertaker. Marvin's brother and friends watched the proceedings in silence.

I could feel Frank's eyes boring into my back all the way back to town.

14

"I'LL GET THAT," I said when the knock came at the door. I crossed the offices of the *Witness*, stopping en route to grab the little revolver I was growing to think of as my "town" weapon.

Lobo Blacke watched me without comment as I carried the gun to the doorway and stood to one side as I asked who was there.

"Leonard," said a boy's voice. "With the beer."

I shrugged. It was time for Leonard. Every evening (except Sunday) at six-thirty, Leonard, the nephew of the proprietor of the Antelope Saloon and Opera House, would deliver a bucket of suds for the consumption of Blacke and (now) myself. It was a pleasant and soothing ritual, and no, we did not between us down a bucket of beer every night. What we didn't drink, Mrs. Sundberg used to leaven bread and to make her marvelous fritter batter.

I reached into my pocket for a coin for the boy (Blacke settled up with his uncle on a weekly basis) and was about to open the door when Blacke said, "Careful. Frank could be standing behind him. He might have a gun on the boy."

"Are you mocking me, Mr. Blacke?"

"Not at all, Mr. Booker. I'm helping you to stay alive in a hostile world."

"Good point," I conceded. "Leonard," I said through the door, "put the beer down and back away from the door."

"Uh, all right."

"Good."

"I'm back now."

Gun ready, still standing off to the side, I threw the door open. No gunfire. I showed myself, looking anxiously left and right. No one there. I tossed the coin to the boy, picked up the beer, and went back inside.

Sitting around Blacke's checker table, we dipped big mugs of amber liquid.

"Well," I said, "I feel extremely foolish."

"You would have felt a damn sight worse than foolish with three or four slugs in you."

"Undeniably true." I raised my glass. "To staying alive in a hostile world."

"Hear, hear," said Blacke, and we drank.

"So," he said, "Marvin was the killer, and Marvin is dead. That's the end of the story, and that's how we print it, right, Booker?"

"I know you by now," I said. "You expect me to say no, don't you? You think the naive tenderfoot is going to get all huffy about Truth and Fairness. You think I'm going to point out that the Real Killer is out there somewhere, and if we let the authorities get away with blaming poor Marvin for it all, the killer will get away scot-free."

Blacke dipped himself another mug of beer.

"Poor Marvin?" he said. "He tried to kill you, twice."

I took a pull on my own. "I know," I said. "And believe me, there was never before, and probably never will be again, a moment in which I admired Sheriff Asa Harlan as much as when he was bringing Marvin down."

"That fool always could shoot. All the connections in his brain go straight to his trigger finger."

"Nonetheless," I went on, "I can't help but think of him as 'poor Marvin.' He was so pitiful and incompetent. He wasn't really cut out to be—not an outlaw, but whatever sort of undesirable citizen he was."

"How about 'varmint'?"

"I have tried," I said with dignity, "to leave that sort of language behind with my dime novels."

Blacke laughed. "Then 'undesirable citizen' will do just fine. I like it. It covers a lot of ground. There's all kinds of citizens I could do with—"

His voice was cut off as though by an axe. His face turned white. His mug slammed down to the table hard enough to spill some. His breath was rapid and shallow and ragged.

"Blacke! What is it, what can I do?"

"Keep your goddam voice down," he snapped. "I'll be okay in a minute."

It was less than a minute. His breath returned to normal, and color returned to his face. The only trace of his ordeal was a thin film of sweat on his forehead, and he took care of that with his handkerchief.

He picked up his beer again and gulped at it almost gratefully while I got a rag and wiped up the spill.

"What in the name of God," I demanded, "was *that*?"

"Nothing."

"That was nothing? Do be so kind as to notify me when you've got *something* scheduled, won't you? I wouldn't want to miss that."

"I was in *pain*, Booker, wasn't that obvious?"

"Tolerably," I conceded. "What I want to know is, pain from what?"

"My legs, dammit. Doesn't seem fair, does it? If I can't move them, why should they hurt?"

Why indeed, I thought. "Have you seen Doctor Mayhew about it?"

"Yeah, before you got here. I pretended I had a cold, so Becky wouldn't know about it. That's all I need. She fusses over me too much as it is."

Blacke turned a glare on me. "And if you let slip a word to her, I swear I'll pack your carcass up on the next train back east."

"It might—it just *might* be better than hanging around here and being shot."

"Oh, *that*," he said scornfully.

I wasn't ready to get into that subject yet. Instead, I asked, "What did the doctor say?"

"He said it happens. He said one of the bullets in my back might be moving around, or my body might be making some 'internal adjustments' like I was the damned printing press or something. He says it's nothing to worry about. I could take laudanum for the pain."

"Why don't you?"

"I hate that stuff. Plus, I never know when the pain is going to hit me, and it never lasts that long. By the time I got to the bottle, I'd be all right. Unless I doped myself up all the time, of course."

"How is it possible that Rebecca doesn't know about this? She sees you as much as anybody. And I'm sure she pays much closer attention."

Blacke was irritated. "Don't trot out your ridiculous theories, all right, Booker? She doesn't know because I control myself. If it gets past the point where I can control myself, I disguise it as a sneezing fit. All right?"

"Sure," I said.

"We'll get back to what we're going to print in the newspaper now, if that's all right with you. All those things you assume I think you're going to say."

"Do you think I am?"

"As a matter of fact, I do."

"Well, as a matter of fact, I am."

"I know you, too, Booker."

"However," I said forcefully.

"Oh?"

"However strongly I feel about Truth and Fairness and catching the real killer, there are some even more important considerations."

"Such as?"

"Such as selling newspapers, for one thing. This week we tell it the way the sheriff wants it. We'll quote him all over the whole front page. We don't say that Marvin killed the professor, we'll just print that the sheriff says he did. Everybody in town—everybody between here and Dakota Territory, north to Montana—will buy a copy to read about it. The professor was a very famous and well-loved man, you know."

"I know."

"Then, when brilliant ex-lawman Lobo Blacke figures out who the real killer is, we print *that*. Then we sell twice as many papers."

Blacke looked me over, nodding.

"Booker, there's a real sneaky streak in you that I've never fully appreciated before."

"There's no reason why we can't be making money while we're chasing killers."

"None at all," he said. "In fact, it makes the whole process a lot more pleasant. And I bet I know your other reason for wanting to print it the sheriff's way."

"What's that?"

"Same as mine. When this killer's nervous, he does things. Dangerous things. Let's let him think all his plans have worked, and that he's safe inside, with no cold winds blowing in on him. I used to do that, you know, let an outlaw figure I'd given up, then circle around his trail and let him come to me. That's what we're going to do with this varmint."

"Will you stop that?"

Blacke grinned.

"At any rate, you're talking as if you know who it is."

He gave me another of his slow nods. "I think I sort of have an idea, yes."

"Who, for God's sake?"

"Nope! Too soon. No proof. Remember, we're working at a disadvantage, here. We not only have to identify the killer, we have to come up with evidence even Asa Harlan can understand."

"We're doomed," I said.

"It's not as bad as all that, my friend. Asa's a puppet, remember, and Lucius Jenkins pulls his strings. Lucius, as you know, is a smart man. If we persuade him, he'll persuade Harlan."

I had a sudden suspicion. "Jenkins and his employees have been awfully prominent in the events of the last few days, haven't they?"

"He's the most prominent man in the territory, after all," Blacke said evenly.

"He was even in town when the railroad car was set on fire."

"What's your point, Booker?"

"This idea you have in mind—this case isn't shaping up as part of your plan to bring Jenkins down, is it?"

"I've been racking my brain to get it to work out that way, but I don't think that's possible. Shame. Still, Lucius will probably love me when this is all over, and that's something gained."

I could see that pursuing this topic was only going to give Blacke further excuses to make cryptic remarks, a pastime he was altogether too fond of.

"All right, then, while we're on the subject of Mr. Jenkins, why did you sit there and let him blather about my being the cause of Marvin's murdering Vessemer?"

"Because I didn't want to hold you up from riding with that posse. You might have learned something important. Which you did."

"More cryptic comments," I muttered.

"What's that?"

"Never mind."

Blacke shrugged it off. "I let him blather," he went on, "because for once, he wasn't the most important man in the situation. Frank is. Now, you've met Frank. Do you think there is any way on earth short of a divine miracle that will change his mind about you?"

"No," I said.

"Neither do I."

"Well, I can't avoid him for the rest of my life."

"I know that. That's why I'm going to take the time right now to teach you how to win a gunfight."

15

BY TUESDAY MORNING, I had learned how to win a gunfight. This did not inspire in me a sense of invulnerability.

For one thing, if anyone in the world but the Great Lobo Blacke had described the technique in question, I would have laughed in his face. I did, in fact, ask Blacke point blank if this was some sort of a macabre joke.

Blacke had just growled at me. "You want to stay alive or not?"

I confessed to being inclined in that direction, so he went on with the lesson, to my increasing disbelief.

For another thing, there was no reason for confidence in the idea that Frank wouldn't just plug me in the back from ambush some night. In this case, Blacke was of some comfort.

"Frank Hastings," he said, "is a little pissant trying to convince himself he's a lion. He'll face you down in Main Street, or in the Antelope, or some place with the biggest possible audience. Make him feel like a man that way."

"Is he fast?" I asked. I was very proud when my voice didn't crack.

"He can get the gun out of the holster," Blacke said. "But he's a fool. He's as big a fool as his little brother was; he's just meaner. And you, Booker, despite your efforts to hide it, are smart. And a smart man can beat a fool every time."

Maybe if I kept saying that to myself over and over again, I could start to believe it.

Just thinking about it made me nervous; I decided to go for a walk.

It was a bad idea. Every doorway had Frank in it, waiting to step out behind me and gun me down. Every window, every rooftop had Frank on it with a rifle, ready to blow my head off. I wanted to walk with my hand on the handle of my gun.

I would have felt much happier if I thought my doom awaited at the end of a knife, or a sword or an axe or a bludgeon. Or poison. Poison would be best.

Since the fire that killed my mother, when she virtually pushed me out of the ground-floor window even as the flames were eating at her body, and I landed in the rose bed outside the window, with pieces of gravel embedding themselves so deeply into the palms of my hand they had to be dug out with tweezers, I have had an unreasoning horror of foreign objects embedding themselves in my body. Bullets terrify me. Just remembering the gravel gives me chills. If, like Blacke, I had to live with two bullets in my back, I would probably never sleep again.

Well, now you know. I never claimed to be a hero.

It was sheer fear of humiliation that kept me from turning tail and going right back to the *Witness*. Not that there was anything to do there; Blacke could print the paper—it was all set in type for tomorrow. I saw it as a place of safety.

Instead, I walked to Doctor Mayhew's office. Stick Witherspoon was there, resting up from loss of blood. And having his wound washed twice daily with carbolic.

I talked to Stick; he thanked me for what I had done for him and told me the doctor had said he'd be fine, in time. I hoped as much would be true for me.

Then I went by Steinmetz's store and did some marketing for Mrs. Sundberg. Steinmetz was holding forth on the Great Manhunt. I didn't begrudge him his glory, but I also didn't want to hang around and listen to it.

When I got back to the office, Rebecca was waiting for me with an envelope, very fine vellum, written on with purple ink. One would expect fine copperplate handwriting on a missive such as this, but instead, in crude block letters, it said:

QUINN BOOKER
THE WITNESS
LE FOUR

Then, in the lower left-hand corner, it read "personal and private."

"How did it get here?" I asked.

"Clothilde brought it." Seeing the no doubt blank expression on my face, Rebecca went on. "Mrs. Jenkins's personal cook. She comes to town on Tuesdays to do some marketing."

That reminded me to put the parcels I was carrying where Mrs. Sundberg would find them.

"Oh, is that the woman I saw a few days ago, yelling at Walker because the vegetables weren't tender enough?"

Rebecca smiled. "That's the one."

I weighed the envelope in my hand, trying to figure out what it was all about. I could hear things sliding around inside, so it wasn't a letter. At least, it wasn't *just* a letter.

It was easy to tell it was from Abigail and that she'd sent it via the cook because Tuesday, the day we put the paper to bed, was not one of her father's days to play checkers with Blacke. Of course, it was also possible that she'd done it this way because she didn't want her father to know she was writing to me.

I thanked Rebecca and went to join Blacke in the pressroom. As I did, Rebecca put a hand on my arm. "Be careful of her."

I told her I'd already reached that conclusion.

Blacke was sitting at his checker table, reading a proof of the front page, all of which, of course, was taken up with the murders and their aftermath.

"You're a good reporter," he said. "A lousy typesetter, but a good reporter. Merton is much better with a composing stick. We've got to find a way to get him to work here more."

"You'll never get him to leave school. His heart is set on being a doctor, like his father."

"Bah," Blacke said. "A doctor can only meddle with people one at a time. A printer can affect thousands."

"I'd never thought of it that way."

"Are you going to open that letter, or are you going to let it come to you in a dream?"

"You mean you haven't steamed it open already?"

"Mrs. Sundberg doesn't like the wheelchair in her kitchen. Tracks up the floor."

"Seriously, it does say 'personal and private.'"

"I know it does. But she went to a certain amount of trouble to get it to you. It makes me curious. Now, if she's just written to tell you she dreams of your big, blue eyes, just keep it to yourself. But it's just possible that she's learned something that will help us understand what's going on around here."

"My eyes," I said, "are green."

Blacke ignored me. "She's a shrewd girl," he said, "and from what you tell me, Marvin was sweet on her, made excuses to be near her. She couldn't help sizing him up in those circumstances. I doubt she holds any more with the official version of things than we do."

"Maybe you're right," I said.

"I won't say I'm *always* right," Blacke said. "Just close enough so as to make no difference."

He's impossible when he gets in a mood like that. I sat down at the other end of the table in Jenkins's checker-playing chair, took out my pocketknife, and slit the envelope.

A piece of stationery that matched the envelope came out, along with a few strips of thick, slick paper, mottled gray and charred at the edges. I picked one up and looked at it.

"This is a piece of a photograph," I said.

"May I see it?" Blacke said.

I grinned. "Since you asked so nicely . . ." I handed the strips over before he started to growl.

While he examined those, I read the letter.

I read the first sentence and burst out laughing.

Blacke looked up over the wire frames of his reading glasses. Now he did growl. "What's so funny?"

"The letter starts, 'Dear Mr. Booker, Feast your devastating green eyes on *these*.' "

A corner of Blacke's mouth went up in a sort of a grin. "See if she has anything to say worth hearing."

I read on, giving Blacke the highlights. "She says that since it is known that the killer took the photograph of poor Marvin—she also calls him 'poor Marvin.' Looks like you're right about her attitude toward the official version, too."

"Naturally," Blacke said. "Go on."

"He took the photograph of poor Marvin and me, so it seems reasonable to assume that he might have taken other photographs away as well."

"I said she was shrewd," Blacke observed.

"She said she sometimes goes for solitude to her father's hunting cabin along the north trail, and she went there this morning and found these in the fireplace when she went to build a fire. She thought I would like to see him."

"You would have really liked to see them before they were burnt," Blacke said.

"That would be hard to arrange, even for someone as shrewd as Abigail Jenkins."

"Very true. Does she say anything else?"

"Oh, yes. She says she only enclosed four scraps to prove her story, and that there are many more smaller ones still in the fireplace. She gives me directions to the place and permission to enter and look around at will. She doesn't tell me how I'm going to get in."

"Hunting cabins are never locked," Blacke said. "Blizzards in the winter and downpours in the summer can come up so suddenly in this country, cabins and lodges are left open so travelers can take refuge. Three or four people a winter in this territory owe their lives to an unlocked cabin door."

"It does my heart good to hear that," I said. "I've been some places where an unlocked cabin would be stripped to the four walls in an hour."

"It's the code of the West," Blacke said with a hand on his heart. "Isn't that what you used to call it?"

I merely sniffed.

"Well," he barked, "what are you waiting for? Get out there and get the rest of those scraps."

"That was my general inclination, but—"

"But nothing. Look at this."

He handed me back one of the fragments. I looked at it carefully.

"What do you see?" he demanded.

"A shoe," I told him. "A simple black shoe. Not too surprising to find a shoe at the bottom edge of a photograph."

"The bottom edge of a photograph," Blacke echoed. "A *portrait* photograph. None of Professor Vessemer's famous nature photos would likely have nicely polished shoes in them."

"True. I'm not sure what it means."

"It means someone killed Vessemer, stole some portraits—pictures *of* somebody, Mr. Booker—took them away, and burned them."

I nodded. "In the unlocked cabin along the trail he probably rode along on the way *to* his ambushes."

"Not only that," Blacke went on. "If he stole and burned the pictures, which, when you think of it, seems to be the entire reason he committed two murders and put your life in danger; and if those pictures are portraits, then those portraits contain a face or faces he does not want us to see. Doesn't want anybody to see them."

"I doubt any of the scraps are going to have faces on them."

"I doubt it, too. But look how much we've figured out from just a shoe."

"It's nice of you to say 'we,' " I observed.

"I'm a nice man. If we can get that far from a shoe, who knows how much some of the other scraps might inspire after a little sitting and thinking?"

"All right. I agree. There's just one thing I'm worried about."

"Yes?"

"What if it's a trap?"

"You suspect Miss Abigail of luring you into a trap?"

"I cast no aspersions on Miss Abigail Jenkins. I'm just trying to survive in a hostile world. I mean, how can I be certain that the letter even came from Miss Jenkins in the first place?"

"May I see the letter?"

I handed it over to him.

"This is a woman's hand," he said. "Grammatical. All spelled right. I think."

"It is," I assured him.

"All right. There may be another woman in this territory who has access to paper this good and purple ink and a woman who can write copperplate *and* spell. Who might even be able to provide the photographs to be burnt. But do you think any of these women are even on *speaking* terms with Frank Hastings, let alone commit forgery and connive at murder for him?"

"No," I admitted. "I'll get Posy and go."

16

IT WAS STILL broad daylight; aside from a few undulations of the patchily snow-covered ground, the territory was flat. There wasn't even enough scrub to hide in. There was simply no place to lay an ambush *from*.

Therefore, there was no reason on earth for that itch between my shoulder blades; it was just there.

I was again wearing Lobo Blacke's gun on my hip. In addition, I was carrying the small revolver in my pocket, and I had a rifle on Posy's saddle. Within another week, I'd add a knife, a cavalry saber, a carbine, and ammunition belts crisscrossed on my chest until I looked like a Mexican bandit.

As Posy ambled along, I peered hard at the ground, seeking tracks that might confirm my theory that this was the route the killer chose last Saturday night to get into position for his ambush, but it was hopeless. Either the ground was too frozen to take identifiable marks, or there had been too much other traffic on this trail since, or I was simply too much an easterner to be able to read tracks worth a damn. Probably a combination of all three.

I was good enough at reading directions, however, to turn off the trail at the right place and see the cabin about a half mile distant.

The itch between my shoulder blades disappeared, replaced with a tightness in my chest. There was nowhere to hide as I approached the cabin. If any ambush were to come, this was the place for it, a shot fired from within the cabin.

I felt better when I saw the horse. A big bay was hitched up to the side of the small building ahead. True, it meant that someone was inside, but it also meant someone was inside who didn't care if I knew it. Someone laying an ambush would have put the horse on the far side of the building.

I was still taking no chances. I drew my gun as soon as I dismounted. I walked up to the rough wooden door of the cabin, turned the knob quietly, threw open the door, and jumped in behind it, gun ready.

Abigail Jenkins screamed.

She was in a bed, covered with a down patchwork quilt, with her bonnet on.

"What did you do that for?" she demanded. "You *frightened* me!"

"I apologize. There are people who do not wish me well, and I didn't know who was in here."

"Why, I said I would meet you here and help with your search in my letter. Didn't I?"

"No, you didn't." I took the letter out of my pocket, walked over to the bed, and gave it to her.

When she had read it, she said, "Imagine that," and slipped out from underneath the covers. She was fully dressed in a riding costume, complete with boots.

"It was cold in here," she explained, pointing to a little cloud of breath for evidence. I was going to start a fire—sweep the scraps out and save them for you, and *then* start a fire—but I thought you might want to see them in place. So I got under the quilt and thought of you while I waited."

I let that pass. "Thank you," I said. "That was the right thing to do."

I had come prepared. I had a little brush and a *Witness* envelope in my pocket. After looking over the fireplace and learning nothing except that photographs had been burned in it, I carefully swept the remains together. I retrieved any unburned fragments, whether they seemed to depict anything or not. Most did not.

"Now can we start a fire?" Abigail asked.

"What? Oh, certainly." I laid paper and timber and stacked fire-wood. Before long, there was a nice little blaze going. Our breath was no longer visible.

"How long have you been here?"

"This time? Perhaps an hour. I came at first this morning, but I was only here long enough to find the burned photographs. I went back immediately to Bellevue to write the note to you and to give it to Clothilde. I caught her just as she was leaving the house. I allowed enough time for the note to reach you, and enough time for you to get here, and came back. But you kept me waiting."

She said it as a statement of fact, without a pout, and without a sign of reproach. It was simply something newsworthy, something to be reported. Miss Abigail was not used to being kept waiting.

"I was not at the office when the letter arrived," I said.

She nodded. "I thought it would be something like that."

"And needless to say, I had no idea you would be here waiting for me."

"Oh. I thought you might suspect. I hope my presence here is a pleasant surprise."

I smiled. "It is, indeed. I hope I haven't disappointed you."

"Not yet."

"I mean to say, if you expected me to exhibit any extraordinary journalistic enterprise, I'm bound to let you know. I've already done what I came to do—sweep up the ashes. I'll bring them back to Blacke to look at."

"One thing I like about this cabin—it doesn't take long for the fire to warm it." She drew off her gloves and removed her bonnet. She began unbuttoning her coat. She had a red velvet dress on underneath.

"It was very shrewd of you to spot the significance."

She arched a dark eyebrow. "For a woman?"

"For anyone."

She reached to her head and pulled pins from her hair. She shook it loose, and it fell in a soft black cataract past her shoulders.

"Except for the ones brought from back east," she said, "virtually every photograph in this area has something to do with poor Mr. Vessemer. It was not a hard connection to make."

She was raking her fingers through her hair, arching her neck in myriad ways as she did so. She seemed to be beckoning.

"So, Miss Jenkins, you are a young lady who knows what she's doing?"

"Always."

"Do you know what you're doing now?"

"Of course. I'm seducing you. Are you immune?"

"No," I said, grabbing for her. "I am not."

She fit beautifully into my arms. I kissed her neck and that soft white throat. By look, by posture, by innuendo, she had been inviting me to take her since the moment we met, and now, she did not attempt to rescind the invitation. Her tongue struck wet fire against mine; her hands were scrabbling at the buttons of my coat.

"Slowly, slowly," I said.

She stepped away from me and took a deep, shuddering breath. "Yes," she said. "Slowly will be better."

I took off my coat and laid it over the table. I removed Lobo Blacke's gunbelt and hung it on the back of the chair. I scooped Abigail up in my arms and carried her to the bed.

Slow it was. Slow, and very delicious. Each little brass button on her frock was the occasion of a long, deep kiss. When the frock was gone, I made the acquaintance of the soft white shoulders as I stroked the soft black hair. I kissed the tops of her breasts and stroked the lovely legs above the cotton stockings.

Sometimes, she would stop me and unbutton or remove something of mine. Improper, unladylike, yes, but incredibly exciting.

I pulled the bow of the lace of her corset, loosened the strings, and parted it like a shell revealing a treasured pearl. Soon, all was gone but the stockings.

"Now," she said. "I want it to be now."

It was astonishing. The smooth but firm grip of her; the fierce points of her breasts digging into my chest. Her sobs, moans, and little screams. The waves of shudders that gripped her one after another, until I joined her in near delirium.

After a while of soft stroking and gentle murmuring, she said, "That was quite satisfactory."

"Thank you."

"For a first attempt." She laughed.

"Oh?" I said. "Are there going to be more?"

She kissed me and did something with her hand simultaneously. "How many afternoons a week can you get away?"

"How long have you been using this for a trysting place?" I countered.

"Since I was sixteen. Marriageable age, but no one suitable to marry. I'm a healthy girl."

"You've shown that."

"So I wait. The men my father approves of aren't sufficiently well bred for my mother's taste; and the ones my mother likes are too poor to suit my father. He's afraid of someone who'll marry me for my money."

"You have so much more to offer than money," I said. "Starting with your—"

"With my what, Mr. Booker?"

"With your clever and uninhibited *mind*, Miss Jenkins, of course." I stroked her head to demonstrate.

"You are a clever man, yourself, Mr. Booker. You have a clever tongue, in whichever way you choose to employ it." She looked me in the eyes for a moment. "Do you think me horribly wanton?"

"Men who think women who have seduced them are horribly wanton are, in my estimation, hypocritical. I do not believe women are supernatural creatures who tempt us beyond our strength against our wills. I believe we must be as willing as they, or nothing need ever happen."

"Do you feel the same way for women?"

"In general. There are added pressures on women. Men may threaten, physically. Or a woman may be dependent on a man for her sustenance, or the sustenance of her children."

"Goodness. You sound like a suffragist."

"Let's not go taking things to extremes, Miss Jenkins." There was something inexpressibly erotic in calling her "Miss Jenkins" in our current situation.

"You are already at extremes. If you or Lobo Blacke tried to print such things in your newspaper—"

I grinned. "This discussion is already much too intimate for the pages of the *Witness*."

"Even leaving aside the intimate parts." She did not suit her actions to her words. She made some adjustments with her intimate parts that nearly distracted me. "My father would try to close you down. He's already said that if statehood comes, and women are still allowed to vote, he will leave Wyoming."

"This sort of talk irritates your father?"

"It drives him wild."

I kissed her. "Then perhaps I will become a suffragist."

"Mmmmmm. Mmm. Why do you say that?"

"Because, forgive me, your father strikes me as the sort of man who should be irritated."

She giggled. It was the first girlish thing I'd known her to do. "I know what you mean. That's probably why I've been irritating him since I was a little girl."

"If he learns of our meeting this afternoon, he might be more irritated than I'd like to have him. I've already got Frank Hastings wishing me dead; I don't need anyone else, especially the most powerful man in this part of the territory."

She embraced me. "Dear Mr. Booker," she said. "Father would not be pleased, but he wouldn't be irritated. Not *that* much, at any rate. He knows I am not the sort of woman to mortify my desires. The blowup about this came some time ago. He was quite vexed, of course, but at last he said there was too much of my mother in me and let it go at that."

She backed away and opened her dark eyes wide. "My mother was once a dance-hall girl, you know. With all that implies."

"Yes, I know."

"So was Blacke's 'niece.' "

"I know that, too. Did your father tell you that?"

"In a way. I overheard it."

"It is very considerate of you not to bandy the news about."

"Oh, I wouldn't do anything to damage her respectability, if that's what she wants." She sighed. "Here we have two dance-hall girls. One who has changed herself into a good woman, and one who's trying to be a Great Lady, and I, who would have made a sublime dance-hall girl—I can even dance—will never get the opportunity."

Something occurred to me. "Abigail," I said, "why did you come out here this morning? Did you come here to meet someone?"

"My, that *would* be wanton, even for me. Why? Are you jealous?"

"I want to know," I said, "who knows about the scraps of photograph."

"Oh. How disappointing. Rest easy, Mr. Booker. I have not used this—or anyplace else, come to that—as a trysting place in over a year. And why I'm telling you this is more than I can say."

"Why did you come out here, then?"

"You won't rest content until you surprise all my embarrassing secrets, will you?" She put her hand to the side of my face. "I come here, Mr. Booker, to write poetry. Very personal poetry that will never be published, or read by a living soul except myself, and perhaps the man I marry. If I love him very much." She gave a mock sigh. "That, alas, does not seem likely."

"Why not? As capable as you are at most things, you should be capable of love."

"Not yet. Attraction, yes. Near obsession—well, you're here, aren't you? But love? I don't know."

She started to laugh, a good strong laugh, womanly but not ladylike. It made parts of her wiggle in fascinating, complex patterns.

"What's so funny?" I asked.

"It just occurred to me who *would* be irritated enough to kill on learning what we've been up to this afternoon."

"Who's that?"

"My mother. She has her heart set on my marrying Sir Peter. The idea of moving to England as the mother of Lady Melling nearly makes her swoon."

"Somehow, I can't see your father in England."

"As far as my mother is concerned, father may have served his purpose. I'm sure her plan is to marry me off to the baronet, come to 'see me safely settled,' and then just never return. If my father were to be . . . irritated, well, my mother has lived off one rich man in America, she'd have no qualms about living off another across the sea. Especially if a chance to meet the queen came with it."

"I see. All it takes is your cooperation. Which she does not have."

"Not yet. I may decide the life of a lady in a civilized land might be worth the boredom and the company of a man who leaves me cold in every imaginable way."

"Have you and Sir Peter . . . ?"

"No. For one thing, he's been housebound until recently, and for another, perhaps I shouldn't have said he leaves me cold. In that way, he finds me cold. Though he doesn't seem to realize it."

Suddenly, she rolled herself on top of me, kissed me deeply, and said, "Do you know that I've never been to a civilized land? Unless you want to count St. Louis."

"St. Louis is fairly civilized," I conceded.

"I was only a little girl when we went there. Where have you been?"

"Well, I grew up in New York."

"I know that. Is it wonderful?"

I smiled. "The place you grow up in is never wonderful. It's just home. A great many people find the Wyoming Territory wonderful in the extreme."

"They," she said, "are welcome to it. Where else have you been?"

"Well, I came through St. Louis on the way here."

"That's *not* wonderful."

"No, just civilized. I've been to Boston, Philadelphia, Washington. Then, when my grandparents took me to Europe, I visited London, Paris, Madrid, Rome . . ."

"Paris! You mustn't tell me that wasn't wonderful."

"It was quite wonderful," I said.

She licked her lips. "Mr. Booker, do you know any . . . any French things?"

"You mean like the Louvre?"

"No. *French* things."

"Oh," I said. "*French* things. Yes. Quite a number. But I didn't learn them in France."

"Show me."

"You're sure, now?"

"Yes."

"Then I'd be delighted." I held her tight, rolled her over, and began to show her a French thing.

For the first time in her life, the Princess of the Plains found herself at a loss. "Oh," she said. "You're going to—there?"

I lifted my eyes to look at her. "That's the idea," I said. "Should I stop?"

"What? Oh. Oh. Oh no. Don't, don't stop. Never, *ever* stop."

OF COURSE, I eventually had to stop. We both had to stop doing all the things she wanted to learn about. I told her that she barely had time to get back to Bellevue before sundown.

"I suppose you're right, curse it," she said. She slipped out from under the quilt and stretched in unconscious grace like some great wild cat, absolutely beautiful in the firelight.

I helped her dress, pulling her stays tight enough for her satisfaction and tying them. Putting her clothes *on* was nearly as arousing as taking them *off*. Obviously, this had to be resisted, or we should be in that cabin until we starved.

I dressed quickly, making sure the gun was loaded and that I still had the fragments in the envelope.

I watched her ride off toward home, then mounted Posy and headed back toward town myself. After a long few hours of standing in the cold, Posy was in a mood to run a little, and I let her have her head. There was no way I would make it to town before dark, but the shorter the distance I had to travel after the sun went down, the better I would like it.

If anything other than imagination stalked me home, I failed to detect it, and I reached the *Witness* building just in time for dinner.

The atmosphere at the meal was decidedly cool. At one point, Blacke asked me if I had gotten what I'd gone for. Rebecca didn't address two words to me. If Merton Mayhew hadn't been eating with us (he was bundling papers after they came off the press, and generally helping

Blacke around the office), I would have spent the entire meal in Coventry.

Afterward, I went to the pressroom, took off my jacket, put on an apron, and started helping Blacke with the pressrun. Things went much faster that way, and I felt a little guilty about being away all afternoon.

That was the point at which Blacke asked me why I'd been gone so long. Sometimes I think he can read my mind.

"Miss Jenkins met me at the cabin. It was such a beautiful afternoon, we thought we'd go for a ride."

Blacke added ink. He had a smudge of it under one eye—it made him look as though he'd been in a fight. He grunted.

"I'll bet you did," he said. "Did you have a good time?"

"It was exhilarating."

"I'll bet," Blacke said again.

We worked on for a time in silence. Sometimes, Merton would whistle. His favorite tune appeared to be "Believe Me, If All the Endearing Young Charms." Either that, or it was all he could whistle.

"Excuse me, Blacke," I said after I could endure the recital no longer. "Don't you want to look at what I've brought back from the cabin?"

"You mean the ashes?"

I told him that was what I meant.

"Very much so," he said, "but I have a newspaper to print. As soon as the pressrun is sufficient to cover our subscribers, we'll take a look."

The formality of his usually colorful language told me I was still in Coventry. The only thing to do was to listen to Mr. Foster's composition as performed by young Mr. Merton, and to wait things out.

We were almost through printing enough copies to cover our list when Blacke said, "Booker, did it ever occur to you to look for your riding companions closer to home?"

"What are you talking about?"

"Becky."

"Rebecca?"

"Rebecca. My . . . niece. She's spending so much time taking care of a crippled old crock, she's wasting away from lack of . . . exercise. And she used to get a lot."

I went cold with anger. This was too much, even from the great Lobo Blacke.

"I see," I said. "Is this the true reason you brought me out here? To keep your niece exercised?"

"Of course not," he said. "What do you take me for?"

"What do you take *me* for?" I countered.

"Well, after this afternoon—"

Merton looked up from his paper bundles.

"Excuse me, Mr. Blacke, Mr. Booker," he said. "But I don't see that there's anything to get upset over. The next time Mr. Booker wants to go for riding, he can ask Miss Abigail *and* Miss Rebecca to come with him."

Blacke looked at me with his eyes twinkling and his lips tight. I had trouble controlling laughter myself.

"In fact," Merton went on, "I wouldn't mind joining the party myself."

So much for self-control. Blacke and I exploded into gales of laughter so loud that Mrs. Sundberg and Rebecca came out to see if things were all right. I was terrified that Merton would explain in embarrassing detail, but he simply said we'd been quarreling but seemed to have made up. Mrs. Sundberg shrugged and went back to her dishes; Rebecca said she was pleased—discord in a house was unhealthy—then stalked away leaving palpable clouds of disdain in her wake.

Her distress sobered Blacke in a hurry, but his anger was gone. "Booker my friend, we need to have a talk."

The talk wasn't too long in coming. We finished up the first absolutely necessary part of the pressrun and, leaving Merton behind to bundle up papers, he and I repaired to his inner office.

I had remembered to take the envelope from my jacket pocket before leaving the pressroom.

"Let me have that," Blacke said.

I handed it over. He took a piece of newsprint, laid it across his desk, then poured the contents of the envelope out. He put on his glasses and enlisted the aid of the lens of a burning glass as well.

"I assume you've already looked at these," he said.

"Briefly. Without a glass. I didn't notice anything."

He looked at a few more pieces before he spoke.

"Do you know why you didn't notice anything?"

"Because I'm slovenly in my mental habits?"

"No. I like that word, though. Slovenly. I'll have to pull that one on

Jenkins. 'I have whupped your ass at this checker game, Lucius, because your play was slovenly.' That'll be good."

"I suppose you're going to say I didn't notice anything because my mind was on other things."

"No, dammit. I can't really blame you for that. I know that wench. If she wants your mind on other things, it will be on other things."

He leaned back in his wheelchair, rubbed his eyes, and sighed. "No," he said, "the reason you didn't notice anything is simple. There's nothing here to notice. Nothing but background on any of the remaining scraps. I'll admit that the shade and what do you call it—the grain—matches the ones on the other pictures. It's a pretty sure bet that these are all from the same photographs. All we have to decide now is whether Miss Abigail planned the whole thing."

"What do you mean?"

"That she burnt up some of her own photographs just to provide a reason to get you out there."

"You flatter me, Blacke. However, photographs aren't something anyone can just burn without their being missed, you know. Even for a rich man like Jenkins, photographs are hard to come by and expensive. Vessemer was only in town for a few days each November. And Mrs. Jenkins—I suspect she keeps a mental inventory of every photograph in the house."

"I suspect you're right. Abigail may be doing this for her own reasons—"

"She's a clever, energetic girl cooped up in a velvet prison and treated like a show pet. She's doing this because it lets her use her brain, Blacke. Nobody's ever encouraged that in her before."

"My, my. How gallantly you spring to defend attacks that were never made. I was saying, she may be doing this for her own reasons, *whatever they may be*, but she seems to be giving us legitimate help."

Blacke sighed again. "Booker, I suppose I owe you an apology for what I said out there."

"I suppose so," I said.

"Don't make this more difficult for me, all right? I haven't made a lot of apologies in my life, and I'm not good at it."

"You really owe the apology to Rebecca. Your idea was lewd and ridiculous."

"How is it ridiculous? I've seen her looking at you. *You* saw her tonight. She figured out what happened, and she was jealous. What other explanation can there be?"

"She was disappointed in me. She doesn't trust Abigail Jenkins, and she warned me against her. I don't entirely trust her either, but Rebecca and I have different definitions of being careful."

"I worry about Rebecca. Don't you like her at all?"

I looked at Blacke. "Have you never had a long-term relationship with a woman?"

"Not day to day, over time. I'd ride into town, find one I liked, paid or not, as she preferred, and rode on in a few days. If I came back to the town, I'd look her up again if she was still there. If not, I'd find somebody else."

"Like a horse getting hay at the livery stable."

"I led a lonely, dangerous life, Booker."

"I understand. My point is, except for specialized circumstances, you have no dealings with women. Suppose I invited Rebecca, under your roof, for some . . . exercise. She'd hate me, and you'd have an excuse to horsewhip me. If I courted her, I would be wasting my time, because she loves you."

"There you go again."

"There I go again, because it's the truth."

"I've seen her looking at you. She's attracted to you."

"And I'm attracted to her; she's lovely. And I admire and respect her. But none of that matters."

Blacke shook his head. "I never realized how complicated life gets when you live it in a house."

With that, he locked the scraps back in the drawer, and we went back to the press. We expected to sell a lot of extra copies the next day.

18

WEDNESDAY DAWNED WARM, and the ground was soft enough to bury Ole Sundberg. His wife had recovered enough poise to go through with it.

There was quite a crowd at the funeral. The Jenkins family was there in severe black, no doubt because Sundberg had been killed coming back from their house, no matter that he hadn't been an invited guest. It was all rather democratic of them, especially of Martha Jenkins. I noticed that Sir Peter Melling had a proprietary hold on Abigail's arm. I tipped my hat as I met the family, and Abigail's eyes twinkled, but otherwise she said nothing but what a sad occasion it was.

It was indeed. Sundberg had been well liked in Le Four, and even some of the drunks from the various saloons in town had gotten cleaned up to see him off. Beckwith provided a good coffin and a nice spot on the hillside. His wife cried softly while Reverend Mortensen eulogized her husband.

It was my first western funeral, and I was impressed with the added sincerity and the decreased fussing that it entailed. Soon it was over, and we all somberly tossed a lump of dirt on the coffin and said our last good-byes. We made our way to the cemetery gates.

"Booker. Over here, you bastard."

Frank was there, staring at me. His eyes were hot and red.

I swallowed my heart and made my voice calm. "Hello, Frank."

"I'm callin' you out, Booker. You killed my brother, and you've got to pay."

"Sheriff Harlan shot your brother, Frank," I said. Meanwhile, my feverish brain was wondering where the sheriff was; I remembered he'd had to go down to Boulder to pick up a fugitive. Frank might have been waiting for something like this to happen.

"He shot him. It was your fault, you and that professor."

"I'm not armed, Frank." Slowly, I pulled my coat back to show him.

"You been wearing a piece." He sounded hurt, as though I'd double-crossed him.

"Nobody wears a gun at a funeral. If you'd like me to thrash you again, I'd be delighted to."

"That won't do. You get a gun. You get one by the end of the day, or I'm going to gun you down where you stand."

Lucius Jenkins's voice came harsh and hard. "Frank, don't be an even bigger fool than your brother. Go back to the ranch and sleep it off."

"You go to hell, Mr. Jenkins."

Shock left no room on Lucius Jenkins's face for anger, at least for a second or two. Then the anger came, cold and tight, and nearly silent.

All the rancher said was, "You're through, Frank."

That's when I learned two things: Frank truly hungered and thirsted to kill me, and I ought to be careful about how I went about irritating Mr. Jenkins.

"Then I'm through," Frank said. "With my brother dead and you doin' nothing about it, I don't want to hang around here, anyway."

Reverend Mortensen, a red-faced former wagon master, said, "Go away, Frank. You won't kill this man; there's too many decent men in this town. We can stop you."

"No!" I said. "I'll fight my own battles. Besides, if we don't have it out, he'll shoot me from ambush. My gun is in town. Frank, I'll meet you in Main Street, in front of the *Witness* in one hour."

"Good," he sneered. "That worthless cripple can take down your dying words."

"One hour." I turned to Blacke. "Let's go back to town."

"Just a minute, Booker." Sir Peter Melling had a hand on my shoulder.

Wonderful, I thought. Now *he* wants to kill me for trifling with the woman he wanted to marry.

"Yes?" I said.

"Well, if I understand things properly, you have just agreed to fight a duel with this fellow."

I smiled in spite of myself. "I guess you could look at it that way."

"Very well. I volunteer to be your second."

"I don't think seconds are much called for around here."

"Yes. Well, I do have a particular and very important service in mind."

Blacke looked up at him with narrowed eyes. "What's that, Sir Peter?"

"I propose to stay with this man Frank until the appointed hour to make sure he doesn't lay an ambush for you."

I was going to say I didn't think it was necessary, but Blacke surprised me.

"I think that's awfully kind of you, Sir Peter. Let it be a fair fight, if a fight's got to come."

"My sentiments exactly."

"You're a true gentleman. Not many Englishmen you meet in the West are like that. Pardon an old man, but most of your countrymen I've known have come out here for richer pickings to steal and wider spaces to run away in."

Sir Peter laughed. "I wish I could say it weren't true. But what of my suggestion? Frank is making his way to his horse."

"You came here with Lucius Jenkins and his family, in the landau, didn't you?"

"I did, but—"

"*A horse!*" Blacke yelled. "Sir Peter needs to borrow a horse to make sure that skunk doesn't bushwhack young Booker! Who'll give him a horse?"

A bay stallion was forthcoming from one of the hands at one of the smaller ranches, who said he'd ride back home in the buckboard with the cook. Since Sir Peter hadn't been on a horse in over half a year, I expected him to need a leg up, but injury and all, he made it smooth and clean into the saddle. Frank had already started off, so Sir Peter only had time to touch the brim of his hat and trot off after him. He sat a horse fine; he certainly rode a western saddle better than I did.

I watched him off, then helped Blacke into the carriage, loaded the wheelchair in the back, and climbed aboard myself. Blacke always insisted on taking the reins, counting on his powerful upper body and his knowledge of horses to compensate for the lack of leverage caused by his inability to brace himself with his legs when reining in.

"Sit up here beside me," he said.

I did so. Rebecca favored me with a look of mixed fury and fear. "You must be insane," she said. "You must both be insane."

Blacke's voice was soothing. "Quiet, Becky. Trust Uncle Louis. That's what Booker's going to do, aren't you, son?"

"Implicitly," I said. "What choice do I have?"

"You could have taken up the reverend's offer of protection."

"Only if I took the next train back east."

"I'm glad you see that. Scared?"

I looked at him. "What do you think?"

"It's natural. Just make sure if you're going to be sick or something, do it before you get out into the street, or sure as shooting, Frank will gun you down while you're retching."

I told him I admired his choice of simile.

"Thank you," he said. "One day, you can explain to me what you just said, but right now, I want to make sure you remember everything I told you."

I rehearsed for him the Lobo Blacke Sure-Fire Can't-Fail Gunfighting Technique for Tenderfeet Who Are Fair Shots but Have Never Drawn a Gun in Their Lives.

"Good," he said. "You do that, and everything will be fine. There's just one more thing I want you to do for me."

"Yes?"

"Don't kill him, okay?"

I started to laugh. I started to laugh at high volume. There might even have been an edge of hysteria to my voice.

"Don't *kill* him? What am I supposed to do? Talk him into renouncing violence and becoming an itinerant preacher? Crease his head so as to induce amnesia, and make him forget he wants to kill me?"

"I'm serious about this. If you kill him, you'll feel bad. You're the kind that would. And don't give him amnesia, either. I want him to know you *could* have killed him, but didn't. I want him to know that you are now all that stands between him and ten years' busting rocks at the territorial prison. I want him to talk to me about everything he's learned working for Lucius."

"I see."

Blacke was smug. "I thought you would. Just wound him up a little; keep him lying in Doc Mayhew's for a couple of months, thinking things over."

"I'll do my best."

Blacke nodded. "That's all a man can ask," he said.

I started laughing again.

19

M E N   O N   T H E I R way to face death rarely wear grins on their faces, so I suppose my riding into town with a big one stuck on my face (totally the result of Blacke's ridiculous confidence in the value of his own advice as executed by myself) must have been an impressive sight.

The people of Le Four certainly seemed to be impressed by it. If word got back to Frank, it might have unsettled him. I hoped so.

There were a remarkable number of people in the street as I rode to town.

"If you want to see insane people, Rebecca, look at your fellow citizens."

"It's just morbid curiosity," she said.

"Morbid is the word. 'Having to do with death.' I mean, I *have* to be out in this street facing bullets."

"You do not," she said. "It's madness."

I more or less agreed with her last point, but it was best not to say so. I simply said, "I won't argue. I was just pointing out the crowds. I don't begrudge them their entertainment, but don't they know that bullets are likely to go anywhere? The undertaker might be able to retire."

"They'll all be safely indoors when the time comes," Blacke said. He wasn't being humorous now; in fact, it seemed to take an active effort of will on his part to shake himself loose from his reverie long enough to speak even those brief words.

When we got to the office, Merton Mayhew was there.

"Mr. Blacke!" he said. "I've been working the crowd, selling papers. We've sold out the whole edition!"

Blacke roused himself enough to ask, "Did you save some copies for the morgue?"

The morgue, I thought. Well, one way or another, Saturday's edition was likely to be another sellout. It occurred to me I'd better win this damnable gunfight, or Blacke, Rebecca, and Merton would have to print the whole thing alone.

That brought another grin, which lasted just long enough for Blacke to wheel himself over to the cabinet, unlock it, and get his gun and gunbelt for me.

He put it in my hands, and once I felt the slickness of old, oiled leather and the weight of the metal, my face forgot all it knew about grinning.

I held it for a moment, looking at it as if it were some kind of strange, frightening breast. Then I tightened my lips and let the beast embrace me. It settled there as if it knew that was where it was supposed to be.

Merton watched me do this. His young eyes looked as though they would burn their way right through his head.

"Then it's true," he said. "What everybody's been saying is true. Mr. Booker's going out to face Frank. Do you think you can take him, Mr. Booker?"

Blacke said, "Shut up, boy."

"What? Oh, right. Right. Sorry. Of course you can." Merton disappeared somewhere, and I was just as glad.

"What time is it?" I asked.

"Five minutes," Blacke said.

"Might as well get out there," I said.

"Not yet," Blacke told me. "The sun's high enough in the sky so as to make no difference which end of the street you're taking. And it's good to wait until the last second you possibly can before turning up."

He wanted me to ask why, so I did. I was surprised to learn that my voice still worked.

"Because every single man alive facing a gunfight is scared. I don't care who he is or how fast, he knows that anything can happen and luck alone can kill him."

"Mr. Blacke," I said, "you don't have to tell me that."

He made a face of scorn. "What, you? You're safe as a church. It's

Frank I'm talking about. He'll ride into town with the Englishman, and he'll get ready, and he'll wait for you. Maybe he'll call for you. When you don't show right away, a part of his brain and his heart will start thinking you're backing out; that he can get away without facing a gun without *looking* like he was glad it happened that way.

"Then, when you *do* step into the street, his heart will sink just that little bit to give you an edge."

"Good God," I said, "another edge. He doesn't have a chance." I licked my lips.

"Not a prayer," Blacke said.

"Well, save a few prayers for me, just in case. How much time, now?"

"Two minutes."

Just then, there was a noise from outside. It wasn't a shout, exactly, sort of a loud collective sigh. This was followed by the sound of footsteps.

"He's here," Blacke said. "The crowd is taking cover. Cut that out, girl."

Rebecca sniffed. I hadn't even noticed she'd been crying.

"I guess it's time," I said.

"Not yet," Blacke said. "One more minute."

Just as that minute—the longest minute since the ancients noticed shadows moving across the ground—just as that minute was up, the door of the *Witness* office opened, and Sir Peter Melling walked in.

"He's here," he said needlessly. "I feel obliged to warn you that he seems awfully confident."

When a man has committed to play a role, there is something that compels him to follow it, no matter how little he feels like doing so. That compulsion was on me now.

"Then he's in for quite a surprise, isn't he?"

Sir Peter smiled and clapped me on the back. "That's the spirit," he said.

I looked at Blacke. "Now?" I said.

"Now."

I said I'd be back in a few minutes and headed for the door.

Becky said, "Wait!" and came to me and gave me a quick, warm kiss on the mouth. "Come back in one piece, you lunatic."

I went out into the street.

Frank had tethered his horse down Main Street, in front of Doctor Mayhew's house. He looked at me and yelled, "Ready?"

"I'm ready," I said.

I saw no signs of his heart sinking as we began to walk toward each other, narrowing the sixty yards or so that stood between us, but Blacke had been right about one thing—all the citizens were off the street. I supposed the braver were looking from second-floor windows. A glance would have told me, but I was following Blacke's advice. *Never take your eyes off his gun hand.*

I could see it, not swinging as he walked, bent slightly at the wrist like a snake hanging from a tree. I'm sure my arm looked the same to him.

It was cold. It had been warmer at the cemetery, but it was cold now. I could feel it in my fingers and in my face. When I had been writing dime novels, all my gunfights had taken place under a hot, blazing sun, not the cold yellow dot in the sky that looked down on us now.

About twenty yards apart, we stopped walking.

I swallowed, once. I kept my eye on his hand.

It moved. I had nothing to fall back on but blind faith in Blacke's advice.

As he had told me to, I grabbed my gun and pulled the trigger while it was still in the holster. I could feel the heat of the blast down my leg as the bullet bored a hole in the leather and buried itself in the ground.

I heard the crack of another shot, but it didn't pass close enough to me for me to hear the whiz of it going by.

Blacke had been right. By God, Blacke had been right.

Not having to clear leather gave me the time to get off the first shot. *Hearing that shot so fast,* Blacke had said, *he'll be so busy wondering if he's dead or alive he won't have time to aim.*

Because the secret to winning a gunfight was not drawing the gun first, it was taking time to aim. So said Lobo Blacke, who ought to know.

While Frank was wasting his first shot, I was able to get my gun out and aim. After that, it was just like being back on the target range with my father at the Point.

I could have killed him. Though I shame to admit it, I even wanted to. All my fear was gone, replaced by a cool, exhilarating feeling of absolute power. It lasted but a split second, but I shall never forget it as long as I live.

But Lobo Blacke had said not to kill him, so as Frank was preparing to fire again, I shifted my aim a fraction of an inch, and shot him in the right shoulder instead of the chest. Then, to make sure he wouldn't be a nuisance for a while, I shot him in the right leg.

Everything seemed to take forever. Events that must have transpired while mere seconds elapsed last hours in my memory. I see Frank falling with a look on his face not of pain, or even of shock, but of betrayal, as though I had badly let him down in some way. And, I suppose, in one way I did.

The pain reached his face as he hit the ground, contorting it as he tried to cover his wounds.

His first cry of anguish broke the spell and brought time back on its proper track once more. I still held Lobo Blacke's gun in my hand. I had to; the holster was ruined. I'd have to buy him a new one.

As if spirited there by a sorcerer, the crowd had returned to the street. I looked at Frank, rubbing his face in the dirt in pain, and said to no one in particular, "Get him to Doctor Mayhew."

Then I turned around and started going back to the office. I hadn't traveled ten steps when I heard another shot.

I turned and crouched in the same motion. The gun was ready. Frank was lying still in the street now. Blood ran from his head for a second, then oozed, making a greasy red halo in the street.

"Who did that?" I demanded.

"I did," a gruff voice said. I looked to see Lucius Jenkins on the far side of the street, not far from Frank, stepping off the boardwalk. He, too, had a gun in his hand. I fancied I could still see a wisp of smoke coming out of it.

I walked toward him.

"Why?" I demanded. "If I wanted him dead, I could have killed him."

"And wasn't *that* a surprise," Jenkins said. "But you were too soft-hearted. He wanted you dead, Booker, and you turned your back on him too soon. He was reaching for his gun."

"Left-handed?"

"Yeah. Left-handed. Ask anybody."

I took him up on it. He didn't get any ringing endorsements, just a bunch of I think sos and maybes. But nobody was willing to contradict the most powerful man in town, either.

"I suppose the fact that he told you to go to hell in front of the whole town had nothing to do with this."

Jenkins's face never moved. Judging from his total lack of expression, I decided he played the wrong game with Blacke. He should give up checkers and switch to poker.

"Not a thing," he said.

"It seems I made a mistake before. I told Frank nobody goes armed to a funeral. It seems you did."

"I got the gun for myself later. I don't bring guns to funerals, but I sure do bring them to gunfights. You never know."

"No," I said. "I guess you never do."

"I saved your life, Booker."

"Then, sir, accept my gratitude."

"Don't mention it."

I tipped my hat to his wife and daughter. "Mrs. Jenkins," I said. "Miss Jenkins."

Abigail merely nodded demurely in reply, but the fire I'd seen in the midst of a passionate embrace was back in her eyes.

Once again, I turned toward the *Witness* building, something I was more and more coming to think of as home. The crowd parted before me like I was some sort of figure of reverence. Merton Mayhew was there, looking at me with naked hero worship.

"You were great, Mr. Booker."

"Not now, Merton."

He didn't hear me. "What happened to your holster?"

"I said not now."

I pushed the door to the *Witness* as though it were the passage between Hell and Paradise. Coming in, I almost tripped over Lobo Blacke.

"I told you it would work," he said.

"Yes, it certainly worked."

"Mr. Booker," Rebecca said. "Quinn. I'm glad you're all right." She gave me another kiss, a much more sisterly one this time. Apparently, I aroused more tender emotions as a man on my way to die than as a man who had just looked death in the face and survived it. I don't think I will ever understand women.

I thanked her. I was glad she had decided to call me Quinn.

To Blacke, I said, "I think I owe you an apology. I never thought the plan would work."

"I've won my share of gunfights that way," he said. "I wasn't the fastest gun in the West, only the smartest."

"Why didn't you tell me this for the memoirs?"

"There's a lot of things I didn't mention in the memoirs, and you know it. Besides, keeping this little trick quiet was a precaution. I knew it would come in handy, someday. Besides, I didn't want to tarnish my legend."

"You're a scoundrel, Mr. Blacke," I said.

"Perhaps, but you're alive."

"True. Do you know what else happened out there?"

"Merton was watching from the roof. He shouted reports down the stairs."

"Merton," I said.

Merton nearly snapped to attention, excited at being paid attention to by the victorious gunfighter.

"Yes, Mr. Booker?"

"Did you see what happened out there?"

"Yes, sir. Frank was lying there, and you turned to walk away. Then he started to reach for his gun, and Mr. Jenkins shot him. In the head."

"Did you *see* that, son?" Blacke asked. "Did you actually *see* Frank reaching for the gun, or are you just taking Mr. Jenkins's word for it?"

"Well, no. I didn't actually see that. I was looking at Mr. Booker. Wow, you were great. Cool as could be, bam, shoulder, bam, leg. But he must have been reaching for it. Why else would Mr. Jenkins have shot him?"

Blacke was rubbing his chin. "Yeah. Why else?"

Blacke wheeled himself over to the safe, took some money out of it, and handed it to Merton. "There's a little bonus in that, Merton. We couldn't have gotten the paper out without you. Tell you what. Why don't you write up the fight for Saturday's paper?"

"Me?"

"Why not? You're a witness to it, and that is the name of the paper. And you're the only witness we've got."

"But Mr. Booker—"

"Mr. Booker is a participant, not a witness. We may run something from him on the side, 'My First Gunfight,' or something like that. Now, run along and see if your father needs any help."

"I will, Mr. Blacke. Thank you, Mr. Blacke."

He was already running top speed by the time he was out the door.

"That's a good kid," Blacke said. "I like him."

"So do I."

That was all the conversation we had on that subject.

"Are you ready to talk about today?" Blacke asked.

"Sure," I said. "Let me go wash my face."

I went to the washroom and splashed my face with icy water. I rubbed hard. The dead, wooden feeling I had felt since before going outside seemed to be fading.

"Well?" Blacke asked when I rejoined him.

"I didn't see it."

"You know, though. Was Frank going for that gun?"

"I don't see how. I'm sure he wasn't. It was an execution, pure and simple. Jenkins shot him down for telling him to go to hell."

"And to keep him from talking about Jenkins's affairs. Especially to me. Nobody's going to miss Frank; that man was a saddle sore with legs if there ever was one. But you were the only one out there with the right to kill him, and you chose not to do it."

"So what do we do about it?"

Blacke shrugged. "Nothing we can do. Witnesses won't talk against Jenkins, and even if they did, Harlan would never make the arrest."

"So Jenkins gets away with it. It's all over."

"All over," Blacke agreed, "except for the fact that we've still got to figure out who killed Vessemer and Sundberg."

20

"I THOUGHT YOU had an idea about that?" I said.

"I *did* have an idea about it," he said. "Now I'm certain of it."

"It would be nice if you told me who."

"No, it wouldn't. Besides, you should have seen it for yourself. You're the one who told me what to look for; the confirmation came today."

"I've had a lot on my mind," I told him.

That got his bark of a laugh out of him. "So you have, so you have. You did a good job out there today, Booker."

"Thank you. But if you've got a clue, and you've got confirmation, what are we waiting for? Let's go make a citizen's arrest and hand him over to Harlan when he gets back."

"That's the problem," Blacke said.

"What is? Like Jenkins, Harlan won't make the arrest?"

"Not at all. Jenkins is going to be very happy when we finally expose this killer."

"And Harlan will be happy if Jenkins is happy."

"Exactly right. But neither one of them is going to be happy without evidence."

"I thought you said you had confirmation."

"Confirmation of my suspicions? Sure I do. But nothing the killer couldn't lie about and explain. No, we've got to do something."

"Something like what?"

"Something like *think*. Things will be well enough for the time being."

The time being stretched out for days. Two more issues of the *Witness* came and went, but the edition with the story of the gunfight in it sold better. The following Wednesday edition was back to new hats at the general store and twin calves born on Ryerton's farms, and trouble with the Indians out in Dakota.

Blacke was in a mood that suited his name. He grumped around, distracted, no doubt arguing with himself in his head, the way he did. I don't know what all was going on inside there, but one thing was evident: The sides of the debate were evenly matched.

I wasn't much better myself. I was lionized through town as though I had single-handedly cleaned up the West instead of merely pulling a trick on a belligerent fool with delusions of grandeur.

I couldn't so much as buy a slab of bacon for Mrs. Sundberg's pea soup without the butcher telling me how brave and resourceful I was. I was getting quite tired of it, and I said as much to Blacke.

He narrowed his eyes at me, rubbed his chin. "Is that so?"

"Yes. To tell you the truth, I didn't especially enjoy shooting a fellow human being."

"Or even Frank, whom nobody will miss."

"Even him. Then to have everybody treat me as if I've discovered a cure for anthrax or something is a little hard to take."

"Well," Blacke said, "it so happens I'm contemplating sending you on a little trip."

"Oh?"

"Yes. To Minneapolis, to fetch Mr. Vessemer's assistant—what was his name?"

"Henry. Clayton Henry. The professor mentioned it once on the train. Why am I going to fetch him? The poor man has a broken leg."

"He should be getting around on crutches by now. And with Vessemer dead, he'll undoubtedly become the railroad's new official photographer. May take over all of the professor's business."

"I'm sure he will, but why not wait until the man is healthy enough to travel?"

"Photographs."

"You want him to take photographs?"

Blacke shrugged. "I might. The thing is, as far as we can tell, this murder was committed because of photographs, and we don't have enough about them. Henry might be able to give us some idea of what photographs are missing, and when and where they were taken."

"It's certainly possible. When would you want me to go to Minneapolis?"

"Not till after the next edition of the paper. I want to write up your trip."

I looked at him suspiciously. "You're setting a trap."

"What if I am?"

"God bless you. Whoever is behind this has led me to experiences I'd sooner have skipped."

I would have been better off if I'd left that minute. Almost all of the remaining days were spent taking orders from Mrs. Sundberg (a waffle iron), Rebecca (history books), Merton (dime novels—anything and as many as I could carry), and Abigail, who rode into town especially to ask me to get her patterns for gowns of the latest fashions in the East and in Europe. I wasn't really surprised, except by Merton. What did a child who could look out a window and see men fire guns at each other with deadly intent, who could go home and help his father deal with the results of that gunplay, *need* with the false and forced thrills of a dime novel?

I could understand a desire for Nick Carter, or Old Sleuth, whose urban adventures could be accommodated in his imagination without the taint of the knowledge of reality to spoil them. But Merton specifically requested several western titles, though he must have been aware since birth that the West of fiction was a bizarrely concentrated dose of the West of reality.

Still, Merton craved them. He said he wished he could read some of mine. I told him I would write to my old publisher for back numbers, and he was almost as awed as he'd been when I'd shot Frank.

The *Witness* came out and I was packing to leave. I was taking a large suitcase, although I wasn't bringing much with me. I would need the space when I did my impersonation of a pack mule on the way back.

The bell rang in my room. That, I had learned on the day of my arrival (just two weeks ago), was an emergency signal from Lobo Blacke. It had not been used since I'd been there.

I rushed downstairs, fearful that one of the bullets near his spine had shifted and done further damage, or that he was trapped by a fire, or something worse.

Instead, I found him in his little office, drinking cider and laughing at the latest number of the *Witness*.

I entered and asked him what the emergency was.

"Sit down," he said. He laughed some more.

I was a little put out. The train left early enough next morning. "I wasn't aware," I said, "that we'd printed anything of a humorous nature."

"Not on purpose. Merton made a typographical error. He wanted to say, 'Mr. Kirkwood's cabbages are now known as the finest in the Territory,' but instead he put 'not.' "

He looked at my impatient face. "Well, it's a lot funnier if you know Kirkwood. He cares more about his cabbages than he does about his kids."

"I don't think you interrupted my packing to tell me that."

"No. I want you to do something."

That was more like it. "Of course," I said. "What do you want me to do?"

"That's the problem. It's illegal."

"Truly illegal, or illegal to Asa Harlan?"

That made him smile. "It's illegal to about just anybody. I want you to commit a burglary."

"Where?" I leaned forward to hear. He was worried about obtaining evidence; I suspected that I was about to be sent to the address of the person he still refused to name—the person he had decided was the killer. "What do you want me to take?"

"I want you to go to Professor Ned's Pullman and steal his camera."

"Steal his *camera?*"

"That's what I said."

"By all that's holy, *why?*"

"Because I have been thinking about why a man would stand there and let his cigar burn and blister his hand without even trying to make it stop."

"And that makes you want me to steal a camera."

"That's right. Do you think you can do it?"

"I don't know. Except for apples from a neighbor's yard, I've never stolen anything."

"That's the hell of being a cripple," he said without bitterness. "You have to ask others to do things you'd rather do yourself."

"I didn't say I wouldn't do it; I said I didn't know if I could get away with it. I'll give it a try."

"I knew you would."

"I'm not entirely sure that's a compliment, but thanks. Any advice?"

"Nope. Gunfighting is a science, but burglary is an art. Every man must practice it in his own way. I've got a lot of confidence in you, Booker."

"Thanks," I said.

"You can finish packing first, if you want to," he said magnanimously.

"I don't think so. If I get shot or arrested, I won't be going anywhere, anyway, so why bother to pack?"

Blacke said I had a good point and that he'd be available if I wanted to ask his opinion of any possible plan I might come up with before I tried it.

He probably meant it—he would—but I was determined, if I were going to do this, to do it on my own.

I realized by now that Blacke was a master manipulator. He manipulated me into the gunfight with Frank, hoping to get testimony that would constitute the first step of his old friend Jenkins on the road to the gallows. Jenkins himself had kept that from working out, but Blacke was wasting nothing. With his newspaper, and my unwilling assistance, since I was part of that newspaper, he had perpetuated and expanded my ridiculous and unsavory "fame" for some new hidden purpose. Why else have me miss the Prairie Wizard twice, just so he could publicize my departure and the reason I was going?

For all I knew, he was trying to get the killer to make a determined attempt on my life. After close collaboration and several spells of living under the same roof, I believe the old lawman sincerely liked me and cared about my welfare. I also believed he was so devoted to his projects and so confident in his abilities to bring his plans off that he wouldn't hesitate to strap me to the target at a shooting range.

I went upstairs and sat a few moments in the comfortable armchair in my room, thinking. I was too big and too clumsy for stealth; I was opposed by philosophy and nature to knocking the poor railway guard on the head, the way he had been the day Abigail and I put out the fire.

As far as I could see, that left only one choice.

I dressed and went downstairs. From the pantry off the kitchen, I took Mrs. Sundberg's largest picnic basket and a red-checked tablecloth.

Already I was on the road to crime.

I slung the basket over my arm, left the building, and walked whistling down the street. The weather had shown a warming trend. I could see my breath, but the ground was softer than it had been a few days ago, and I was comfortable with my greatcoat unbuttoned.

As I approached the night-deserted station, I sang out for the guard.

My plan was simple: I would be brazen. If Lobo Blacke could exploit my newfound fame, so could I.

"What d'ye want?" the guard demanded. He was an old Irishman named Connor; he was left over from the building of the railroad. Connor's face was a contour map, a legacy of too many nights out in the heat and cold and too many pints of whisky to take his mind off the discomfort. His hair had once been red; now graying, it looked disconcertingly pink in the lamplight of his cabin.

"It's Quinn Booker, Mr. Connor. From the *Witness*."

"Is it, now? Come here, let me have a look at you."

I approached and let him see me.

"Well, it is you, for a fact. What are you doing out this time of night? Say, I saw you with that miserable Frank Hastings. Why'd you let Jenkins have the pleasure of killing the bastard?"

I managed to smile. "I guess I just like to spread the fun around."

Connor wheezed, and I thought he was going to choke, but in fact he was laughing. He laughed until his eyes teared; his complexion became alarmingly red. He said, "Spread the fun around," and started out with another wheeze. After two or three times around he at last subsided, and I told him I'd been sent to fetch something from Mr. Vessemer's car. As he knew, I had discovered both the body and the fact that that railroad car had been the scene of the crime.

Ten minutes later, I was walking away with the camera heavy in the basket on my arm. Connor had even held the lantern for me.

21

ON MY WAY west, I had thought St. Paul a fairly impressive city to be on the middle of the prairie; coming there after a couple of weeks in Le Four, the place seemed like Babylon. I hadn't realized before how much one's impressions depend on the direction you're traveling.

The train trip had been uneventful. I spent a lot of it writing the first part of this memoir, since there was no one close to the equal of the late Professor Vessemer as a conversationalist.

That's not to say there was no conversation on the train, simply that I didn't take much part in it.

For instance, there was one gentleman who was grumbling that he had been in the West six weeks and hadn't once seen a stampede or an Indian attack.

Since these are two of the worst things the westerner can imagine, some of his fellow passengers explained at length, and in colorful detail, why he should be glad he'd been spared those particular spectacles.

"Well, all right," the fellow had grudgingly conceded. "But in all that time, I didn't even witness *one single gunfight*."

That was when I decided to see if the dining car had opened yet.

I got off the train in St. Paul and went to the headquarters of the railroad. I ran into a reluctance on the part of the workers there even to acknowledge Mr. Clayton Henry as an employee, let alone part with his address. But the ferreting out of information, city-style, was what I had been trained in; I spread a few half eagles around and wound up almost carried to the man's house like visiting royalty.

Mr. Henry lived across the river in Minneapolis. Now, the river in this instance is the mighty Mississippi, but readers of Mr. Mark Twain may be surprised to know that in the northern latitudes, the Father of Waters is in fact a creek you could swim if it were warm enough.

In any case, a cab brought me across a bridge that was only slightly more convenient than having the horse jump across, and on through town until we reached a nice neighborhood of small houses on neat, square lawns.

As I approached the front door, I heard beautiful music. Someone inside was making a violin sing. I almost hesitated to knock.

When duty compelled me to knock anyway, the knock was ignored. I waited until the end of the piece and knocked again.

This time the door was opened. Clayton Henry said, "Why do you interrupt me? I am playing a tribute to my friend." He had a heavy cast on his left leg and was leaning on crutches under his shoulders.

"I am sorry to interrupt you. The music was beautiful."

He sniffed. "And how could *you* appreciate it?"

"I have never heard better in New York or London," I said.

"No," he said. "If you have ever *been* to New York or London."

I was rapidly coming to the conclusion that Mr. Clayton Henry was an irksome boor, but I was forgiving him much for his playing—and, of course, because Lobo Blacke said he needed him.

I decided to start again.

"My name is Quinn Booker. I—"

"I didn't ask what your name is. I ask why you interrupt me."

"I interrupt you to speak to you civilly, if you can manage it, about your friend, and mine, Professor Vessemer."

"You knew Vessemer?"

"Briefly, but we got along. I spoke to him the night he died. I found his body."

Henry's hair had a tendency to gather in small spikes and stick up at odd angles from his head, giving him the look of having a baby porcupine sitting on top of his head. He ran a firm hand over the top of his head and turned it back into a head of hair for a few seconds. Then the tendrils began to spring up again. It was quite fascinating to see.

Henry was staring at me even more intently than I at him. After a few seconds, he made a humming noise in his throat and said, "You have attained a rare achievement, Mr. . . . . Booker, was it?"

"That's right."

"A very rare achievement. You have interested me. Please come in."

He brought me to a room absolutely filled with clutter. Music scores, books, periodicals, pieces of bone, specimens in spirits—the room was filled with them. There was only one chair whose seat was visible. A music stand was in front of it, and a violin and bow rested on the velvet cushion like jewels.

Henry hobbled over, dropped his crutches, picked up the instrument, and plunked his lanky body heavily in the chair.

"Very well," he said. "You have come to talk with me. Civilly. Do so. Tell me what you know about Edward Vessemer."

I gave him a fairly detailed outline of recent events in Le Four. I left out a few things—how I spend my afternoons, for instance, I judged to be none of his business. But by the end, he was as up-to-date as I was; ahead of everyone but Lobo Blacke and the killer.

Apparently, I held his interest. With a nod that shook a few more spikes free, he said, "So you shot this Frank?"

"I had no choice."

"I was tempted to shoot him every time Vessemer took us to that godforsaken outpost. You actually left the East to live there by choice? Amazing."

Idly, he picked at the strings of his instrument. "And you are saying that the person the sheriff and everyone else agrees killed Edward did not in fact do it?"

"For the reasons I gave you, yes."

"They may be cogent. What I fail to understand is why you have come to *me*."

"I've come to ask you to move forward your trip to Le Four. To come back with me on tomorrow's train."

"My what?"

"You'll have to return to retrieve the special Pullman, won't you? I don't suppose the railroad will choose anyone else to succeed Vessemer."

The look on Henry's face suggested he'd gotten a bad oyster.

"No, no, no, no, no! You don't understand. I am not a photographer; I assisted Edward because I admired him, and because I needed a chance to earn my bread in this miserable world."

"You're right. I don't understand."

"In Edward Vessemer, I found a true equal; a man with the soul of an artist. But he, you see, owned the future. He was the master of a *new* art. I am only the master of old arts, arts that are dying."

He pointed to a painting on the wall, a portrait of a beautiful and haughty woman in the prime of life. I had seen worse in museums and said so.

"Bah!" Henry said. "With men like my friend perfecting the art of photography, what is the use of portrait painting? In minutes, he could capture essences that took me weeks."

He held up the violin. "Again, this. I am a passable practitioner. I am not the best in the world, but I brought a modicum of joy to those rare places where beautiful music was appreciated.

"But that, too, has been destroyed. And as jest from the gods, it has been destroyed by a teacher of the deaf."

"I beg your pardon?"

"A Mr. Bell. I have read of his exhibit recently at the Philadelphia exhibition. A device he calls the telephone."

"Oh, yes. I saw it. I was there the day Dom Pedro of Brazil said, 'It talks!' "

"It does more than that, curse it. Do you know what this Bell proposes to do? He plans to put these telephone devices in homes and concert halls, and let musicians play simultaneously for multitudes across the country over his wires.

"What need will there be then for more than one violinist; more than one pianist; more than one tenor? When the public can hear the best, why should they bother with others?"

"But it will take years and years for just the well-populated areas of the country to be wired in that way. You might play for decades."

"I am not temperamentally suited," he said, "to devoting decades to a doomed enterprise. Edward was kind enough to allow me to become, in a small way, an acolyte in the temple of the future. I can take a photograph; I can develop and print a photograph. But it will never be art. My arts, Mr. Booker, are moribund. My only use for them now is, fittingly, to use them to mourn the dead."

He hung his head.

"There's another art you can assist in, you know."

"And what is that?"

"It's an art that can never be outmoded, so long as men are men. The art of bringing the criminal to justice."

"I see. And are you such an artist?"

"No, Mr. Henry, I am not. But the man I work for, Louis Bowman Blacke, is—though he'd scoff at the characterization. He has sent me to fetch you, because he believes with your help he can bring the man who killed your friend and mine—and his, for that matter—to the gallows. Won't you trust him?"

Henry scowled more fiercely than ever; he even made a noise deep in his throat that harmonized with the bizarre tune he plucked on his violin.

Finally, he said, "Very well. I agree to drag my shattered limb to that ridiculous town one more time. For justice to my friend. And for one other reason. Do you know what that reason is?"

"To tell you the truth, sir, as long as you're coming I don't much care."

He sniffed. "I shall tell you anyway. I am going to see the look on Lobo Blacke's face when I tell him you called him an artist."

22

IT WAS ARRANGED that I should send a cab for Mr. Henry and meet him at the station the next morning. We also arranged that since the railroad hadn't gotten around to authorizing his trip, the expenses and a small emolument would be the responsibility of Louis Bowman Blacke.

A telegram was waiting for me at the hotel. Since only Blacke knew I was here, I tore it open eagerly. Perhaps there had been a break in the case.

Imagine my surprise when it turned out to be another shopping list. I was to have Mr. Henry obtain, at my expense, all the equipment needed to develop a photograph. I was to wire if I needed more money.

It was like him. He *wanted* me to wire him because he knew I wouldn't ask for more money; I would ask what the devil was going on; what was wrong with the carful of equipment sitting in the railyard in Le Four.

He would read that. Then he would chuckle and wire me more money.

I cursed under my breath and wished, art or no art, that Mr. Bell's telephone device was already in universal use. Then I could simply establish contact with Clayton Henry, obtain a list of what was needed, and get it.

As it was, I had to go all the way back across the river, bother the cantankerous Mr. Henry once more (if he felt any joy at seeing me again, he managed to contain it), then back to commence my shopping.

With the loss of time, and the extra items to track down, I barely got it all done before the stores closed. I also found a book emporium in Minneapolis, where a very thin man named Stilwell sold me the items on Merton's list. I spent most of the evening trying to get everything packed. Even with the extra trunk I had purchased, I had no room to spare.

Clayton Henry wore his usual sour look and spiky hair as he crutched his way toward the train the next morning. Eyeing my mound of luggage, he said, "When I itemized that equipment for you, I don't believe I said anything about obtaining sufficient materials to build another Pullman car."

"Someday in the future," I told him, "I'll reflect on your remark, and then I will laugh. Right now, I'm not in the mood."

Outrageous bribery to two porters got the stuff on the train. A hand up got Henry aboard as well, and then, by God, I got him to Le Four. He complained every waking moment of the trip, but I got him there.

It was raining in Le Four when we arrived. We were met at the train this time not by Rebecca but by a grim-faced Sheriff Asa Harlan.

I assumed he was going to arrest me for some trumped-up charges having to do with the now legendary Booker-Hastings gunfight, but I was wrong.

"Hello, Booker," he said gruffly.

I was helping Henry down from the train. When he was safely down on the platform, I handed him his crutches and turned to the sheriff. "Hello, Mr. Harlan," I sighed. "I'll go with you, if you want, but I ask you to let me get Mr. Henry, who you see has a broken leg, safely to the *Witness* office. Do you know Mr. Henry?"

"We've howdied, but we ain't shook."

"Quite," Henry said with the driest possible smile. "Howdy."

The sheriff missed the insult completely, which was just as well.

"Howdy," he said. "Anyway, that's why I'm here. To see you and Mr. Henry and your stuff get to the newspaper."

"That's awfully nice of you, Sheriff."

"Nice don't have nothing to do with it. Blacke swears to me that Mr. Henry and this stuff have something to do with what happened around here, so I plan to keep them nice and safe."

"He did?" My voice almost squeaked. I don't know which idea I found more astonishing—that Blacke had let the brave and accurate-shooting but otherwise inadequate Sheriff Harlan in on his suspicions about the murder of Professor Vessemer, or that the sheriff, who had been convinced he had brought down the killer with a well-placed shot, was taking him seriously.

"Yup," Harlan said. "The other night, somebody strangled Connor, the guard, and burnt up Professor Ned's Pullman. Blacke's afraid whoever did it might have it in for Mr. Henry, too."

"Oh, might he?" Henry asked. He gave me a very dirty look, in response to which I could only shrug.

"Yup. And there's been too many murders in my jurisdiction already. I don't like 'em. They look bad on my record."

The sheriff gave a whistle, and an army of helpers materialized as from nowhere to carry the goods to the office. I took a short walk down the platform from where I could see the blackened ruin that had once been Edward Vessemer's home away from home.

Henry had clumped up behind me.

"Great things were done in that railway car," he said. The usual bombast was temporarily missing from his voice, replaced by real emotion. "In its way, its destruction is as great a crime as Edward's murder."

"Then let's go see what we can do about it."

"Indeed. With you and the sheriff to protect me, I think I can make it."

Blacke himself opened the door for us.

"Welcome!" he said. "Glad to be back?"

I said I didn't know. "But I'll tell you one thing," I went on. "The West is getting to me. I felt naked out on Main Street without a gun on."

"Anytime. It's yours now. I had Peretti the cobbler make up a new holster while you were away." He turned his attention to our guest. "Mr. Henry. Thank you for coming. I think I can say I sympathize with your injury more than most people can."

Henry said on the contrary, his condition gave him a new empathy with Blacke. I had to look at the artist twice; I hadn't thought graciousness was in his repertoire.

Blacke offered him refreshment—cider, beer, cool well water. "I can get you some grub, if you like, but I'd really like to get started on our work—things are coming to a head."

"Interesting," I said. "What head? What things?"

"I'll explain later."

"Oh no, you don't get away that easily. What happened at the railway line?"

"Didn't the sheriff tell you?"

"Oh, he told me what happened, but I want to know *what happened.* I feel terrible about Connor. The only time I ever spoke to the man, I tricked him."

"Very simply, the killer has apparently been thinking about photographs as hard as I have."

"You mean he burned up the car to destroy any that might be left?"

"That's what he had in mind," Blacke said. "But I hope the one he wanted most to destroy was one that *wasn't* left."

He spun his wheelchair in the direction of the office safe and spun the dial while he talked.

"And that," he said, "brings us to *you*, Mr. Henry."

"I've come this far. I'm ready."

Blacke pulled the handle and opened the safe. He reached in and grabbed the gleaming mahogany of the camera I had stolen the night before I left.

"Booker, would you come get this and hand it to Mr. Henry?"

I complied. We all handled it like something precious, which, for all sorts of reasons, it was.

"Now, Mr. Henry," Blacke said. "I am pig ignorant about cameras and such, and that object in your hand is so potentially important, I didn't have the guts to find out. Here's the question I brought you all the way out here to answer: Is there a photographic plate in that camera?"

"You must be joking," Henry said.

"My jokes are generally a whole lot funnier and easier to get than this."

"Yes, there is a plate inside this camera. Do you see that the slot is filled? That is the plate. You would pull that tab to remove it."

"Don't remove it now!" Blacke's earnestness almost had him sweating. "Can that plate be developed?"

"Perhaps. The chemicals involved lose their potency over time."

"How much time?"

"It depends. They will last much longer in cold conditions. Edward and I had terrible problems in the summer."

"It's winter now."

"As my broken bone never stops informing me. There is cause for hope."

"Can you develop it now?"

"Of course not. I shall need a room, and I shall need the equipment the young man asked about set up."

Blacke nodded. "I know that. I should have asked, if we get started now, can we have it done by, say, five o'clock this evening?"

"I believe so."

"What's so special about five o'clock?" I asked.

"We have to go out to Bellevue. Mrs. Jenkins is throwing another party. We're all invited, even you, Mr. Henry."

"I hate parties."

It figured that he would, but I had something else on my mind. "Another party? So soon after what happened at the last one? Seems a little lacking in taste to me."

"Why? It wasn't her fault, was it?" Blacke has no capacity for understanding the finer points of proper social conduct. "Still," he said, "Martha seemed worried about that, too. The invitation said something about 'joyous news being its own justification' or some such jumped-up nonsense."

I smiled. "She wore her daughter down. She's going to announce Abigail's engagement to Sir Peter Melling."

"Yeah," Blacke said. He was smiling too. "Yeah. I'll just bet that's what she has in mind."

"So I suppose I ought to go," I said.

"We're all going," Blacke said. "I wouldn't miss this one for the world. Rebecca informed me it would take her the entire day to get ready. Now, if you'll just do what Mr. Henry says, we might be able to make it."

Henry crutched around the ground floor, trying to decide where the equipment should be set up. He finally picked Blacke's sitting room, which had only one window but a table adequate for his needs.

Then I got busy, tacking the black velvet tightly over the window, arranging the reflectors, laying out the chemicals in the order instructed, placing the enameled trays just so, and tongs just so.

Blacke insisted on being in the room while this was going on. In the small room with the wheelchair, with a man on crutches, and me whirling like a dervish attempting to obey commands, he couldn't help being in the way. I might have wished him out of the room except for one thing: He began to explain what was going on with the case.

"You see, Booker, I couldn't get it out of my mind about those burns on Vessemer's hand. Apparently, he just clutched his cigar and let it blister him up good—while he was still alive. You ever been burned, Booker?"

I had never told him how my mother died; how she shielded me and saved me in the fire at the cost of her own life. "Yes," I said. "I have been burned."

"Then you know how much it hurts. Hurts worse than being shot, I can tell you that. I couldn't help thinking a man would have to have a powerful reason to let that happen to him, but I couldn't figure what. Couldn't figure it for the longest time. Other things told me who the killer must be, but those burns bothered me."

"Mr. Booker," Henry said. "I hate to interrupt an artist at work . . ."

So he'd found a chance to get Blacke's reaction. I don't know if he was disappointed or not, since Blacke seemed to quite like it.

". . . but the time has come to remove the clear mantle from the lamp and replace it with the red one. Red light will not damage the photograph."

I did as instructed.

Blacke went on. "Then I thought, what happened just before Vessemer died? He was in a dimly lit room with a man who had waylaid him and forced him to be there. The man was already forcing him to remove some photographs from the files. Vessemer was a smart man—smart enough to know that if the photographs were dangerous, the man who had taken them was equally dangerous. He must have known he was going to die."

I felt, rather than saw, Clayton Henry shudder as he poured chemicals in trays and removed the plate from the camera.

"It seems to be all right," Henry said.

"Good," Blacke said. "Let's just hope it contains what I think it does."

"Which is?" I demanded with decreasing patience.

"The name of the killer. Imagine it, Booker. The man knows he's about to die, but he also knows who the killer is. And he knows he's got a photographic plate in the camera. Didn't you tell me once the word *photograph* was Greek for 'written in fire'?"

" 'Written in light,' " I said.

"All right, written in light. But the light in this instance came from a fire—the coal on the end of his cigar."

"Of course," Henry said. He added some more from a chemical bottle. "Quite ingenious. And quite like Edward."

"You see it, don't you, Booker? Walking around the room, collecting photographs, he opens the shutter of the camera and leaves it open."

"That would work," Henry said. "Edward built a small clockwork mechanism into the camera that kept the shutter open the required length of time. He hated to stand there and do it manually."

"Thank you, Mr. Henry. I had worried about that. But look now. With the shutter open, the only strong source of light in the room is the cigar, which he holds in his mouth, or in his hand. He gets in front of the camera whenever he can, and slowly, so the killer won't notice him doing it—"

"Slowly would work better photographically, as well," Henry said.

"Well, he'd know that, bless him. Slowly, then, for both reasons, he'd trace the name of the killer in the air, as many times as he could, hoping it would be written in fire on the plate, and that we'd have wit enough to develop it and see."

"I'm getting something," Henry said.

I was excited. "Brilliant, Blacke."

"Almost too late. The killer thought of it just one day after I did. If I'd left the camera in there, it would all be gone."

"Here it is," Henry said. "It's faint, but I think legible. Bring it closer to the light, please, Mr. Booker."

I did. And there it was. Written against a field of black in a ghostly, grayish white, were shaky, cloudy shapes that were indeed letters.

" 'TRAB,' " said Clayton Henry. "Does that mean something to you?"

"Trab?" I said. "Trab?" Then it came to me. "It's backwards! Look at the *B* and the *R*. Facing the camera, the writing would come out backwards, just like a mirror. He was trying to write 'BART'!"

"Bart?" Blacke said. "Let me see that." He wheeled over and nearly upset Mr. Henry as he snatched the picture from my hand. "Bart. That's what it says all right. Now all I want to know is, *who the hell is Bart?*"

23

LOBO BLACKE SAT way back in his chair, with his eyes narrow and his lips tight. I had never seen him so angry, even when he talked about his old friend, Lucius Jenkins, and the ambush that had killed the lower half of him.

Lobo Blacke was the kind of man who reserved his worst anger for himself.

It was an hour before I could even bring myself to talk to him. Clayton Henry, tired from the journey, had been shown to the guest room. Mrs. Sundberg, knowing she wouldn't have to cook tonight, was visiting her sister in the next town; they were undoubtedly discussing Mrs. Jenkins's taste. Rebecca was still getting beautiful for the party, a case of gilding the lily if I ever heard of one. Blacke was in his dark reverie, and I was almost afraid to leave him alone. Not because I thought he'd do away with himself or anything—he wasn't that kind of man—but that someone would come in to buy a paper and Blacke would bite his head off.

At last, in tones as conversational as I could manage, I said, "Why couldn't it be someone named Bart?"

Blacke did not bite my head off. He just asked, "Do you know how many men named Bart there are in this territory?"

"No, I don't, and neither do you. How many are there in town?"

"None. That's what I've spent the last hour trying to figure—where's the nearest Bart?"

"I'm glad to see you're not giving up."

"I might as well. A man wouldn't lie when he's trying to name his killer. So the killer is Bart. And that means the killer *isn't* who I've been sure it was." He pounded a fist on the arm of his wheelchair. "Damn it, though, it's got to be. Everything else says so."

"If you don't mind my asking, who *is* this other person you've been so coy about?"

And much to my surprise, he told me.

And then I started to laugh. I must have laughed for ten minutes. Blacke had to threaten to run me down with the wheelchair before I could possess myself enough to tell him why.

After I did, he said, "I'll be a son of a bitch."

"Maybe you won't be so cute next time about telling what's on your mind," I said, though I doubted it.

Blacke looked at the clock. "Come on, there's just about enough time for us to get dressed up fancy and go to the party. We've got some news for people."

We made it in time. Most of the same crowd as last time was at the party, maybe even a few more. Curiosity, I suppose. Also, something new had been added. In addition to the coat-check room, there was a room in which one could check weapons. It was doing great business. Apparently, no one wanted to miss the party, but no one was about to forget the ambushes after the last one, either.

In fact, knowing what was in store that evening, I was disinclined to give up Lobo Blacke's gun (now mine) into the keeping of anyone, let alone one of Lucius Jenkins's servants.

Blacke told me to go ahead and not to worry about it.

"I do worry," I said. "I can't help it. Are you sure you want me to do this?"

"I'm positive. I don't want to make anybody suspicious."

"But what if things get . . . ah . . . unpleasant?"

"I've got very persuasive arguments."

And if he doesn't, I thought, he'll just stubborn the person in question into submission. It was easier to see all the time that what had made him a great lawman was persistence.

Henry had already joined the party, hobbling off in search of wine good enough for his educated palate. Rebecca was bending to fix Blacke's tie, and he was complaining about the attention. Then she stood, removed her cloak, handed it to me, and asked me to check it.

I just stood there for a moment, looking at her.

I confess to certain feelings of dread when I heard she was taking all day in her room to get ready for this. I was afraid some obscure feeling of competition would lead her to re-create the dance-hall girl she once was and had worked so hard to put behind her.

I had wasted my time worrying. It was obvious that Rebecca had spent most of the day deciding not to do much of anything. Her gown was white and showed a certain amount of collarbone; otherwise it was positively demure. In the lights of the big house, I could see as I couldn't before that she had left her lovely face alone—at least as far as male eyes could tell. Her golden hair was simply and beautifully drawn back from her face.

I told her she looked especially beautiful this evening.

She dimpled prettily. "Thank you, Quinn," she said. The unselfconscious use of my given name was disarming. For all of Blacke's seeming interest in throwing us together, I suspected that if Rebecca truly desired me with her, nothing would be able to keep me away.

I confess to very little resistance to the charms of women. But you probably had reached that conclusion on your own by this point.

Rebecca insisted on wheeling Uncle Louis into the ballroom. I waited outside a few seconds, took a deep breath, and entered on my own.

And was immediately beset by the other truly beautiful woman at the gathering, Abigail Jenkins.

She was dressed in her favorite red, her eyes were kohled, and jewelry sparkled from her ears, fingers, neck, and bosom. If Rebecca seemed a sanctifying angel, Abigail seemed a bewitching imp.

"Mr. Booker," she said. "How wonderful that you returned in time."

"Always a pleasure to see you, Miss Jenkins."

Still smiling, she dropped her voice conspiratorially. "They have worn me down; I am to marry Sir Peter. Let's you and I run away together."

"You don't mean that," I said.

"Not yet," she conceded. "But after three or four more glasses of wine, I may be screaming for someone to rescue me."

"And you may get it," I said."

"What do you mean by that?"

"You'll see. Are you taken for this dance?"

"Only by you, Mr. Booker."

We swept off onto the floor, the pleasure of having my arms around her marred only by what I knew was to come this evening.

The music ended. Abigail was swept off in a swirl of admirers.

Rebecca had a swirl of her own. She seemed to be enjoying herself. I noticed, as evening passed by, that she never danced with the same man twice.

I looked around for Blacke to see if he needed anything, and saw him being almost smothered by the Amazonian form of Martha Jenkins. To judge from her face, Blacke was keeping her amused with a nonstop flow of charming repartee.

Even Sheriff Harlan was at the party, looking about as comfortable in his evening dress as a rooster in boots. Still, Rebecca gave him a dance, as she did Doctor Mayhew. If Merton had only been there, he would have swooned in ecstasy when his turn came. Sir Peter Melling had kind words for her. Lucius Jenkins, who at the last party had suffered uncomfortably around the floor only with his wife and his daughter, was persuaded to squire Rebecca around.

"She's added a bit of fresh charm to the gathering, hasn't she?"

I turned around to see Sir Peter Melling. I noticed the baronet had the disconcerting habit of appearing beside you without attracting your notice. It was especially unsettling because he was so big. Something that size should make some noise.

"She's quite a girl," I conceded.

"I must tell Mr. Blacke that he does the whole town a disservice when he hides his niece away from us."

"I think it's her choice, actually. In any case, Sir Peter, there are strong suspicions about this evening that you are to be congratulated."

He smiled broadly. "Are there now? Well, one mustn't take anyone for granted."

A little while later, I saw a small gap in the crowd around Rebecca. Boldly, I slipped through, and I asked her to dance.

"I thought you've been avoiding me, Quinn."

"I didn't want to get trampled by your admirers."

"I *like* it, Quinn. I never dreamed I would like it so much. To have men treat me as a prize to be won rather than as a commodity to be purchased . . . it's wonderful."

"Good for you," I said.

"The only flaw in the situation is that I've been working."

"Oh?"

"Yes. Tell Uncle Louis, if you get a chance, that the person he asked about is carrying the only gun in the place, aside from the sheriff, so far as I've been able to tell."

Beautiful, virtuous, and clever. I was tempted to kiss her, but I fought it down.

I was also tempted to go out to the vestibule and get my gun. This was no hotheaded fool like Frank we were talking about now; this was a cold-blooded killer.

I waited for Mrs. Jenkins to turn Blacke loose, waited while she swooped down on me for a brief gush, then reported what Rebecca had told me. Then, *sotto voce*, I told him I was going to get my gun.

"No," he said.

"Yes."

"No."

"Yes, dammit."

"For Christ's sake, Booker, I coach you through one gunfight, and suddenly you think you're Wild Bill Hickok."

"Or you?"

"If you'll have it that way, take it that way."

"Look, Blacke, I'm not saying I'm the best conceivable person to have armed in this situation, I'm just the only one. I'm going to—"

A cutting gesture with his hand stopped my urgent whisper. "It's too late, anyway," he said.

Lucius Jenkins was being pushed out to the middle of the floor by his wife. She left him there and retreated to the perimeter, standing by her daughter and Sir Peter like someone guarding a pair of trophies.

Jenkins cleared his throat, then began.

"Ladies and gentlemen, it's an honor—an honor and a privilege and, uh, a pleasure for you all to be here this evening. I mean, it's all those things for me. Me and my family."

It was a good thing his fortune didn't rest on his prowess as a public speaker.

"I have a happy announcement to make. My—"

"Just a second, Lucius," Lobo Blacke said.

"For God's sake, Louis, can't it wait?"

"It had better not," Blacke said. "You'll be glad I interrupted, when I'm through. There are a few things that need to be cleared up."

"Like what the big idea of messing up my wife's party is, right, Louis?"

"She'll thank me, too. You see, we now know the killer of Professor Vessemer and Ole Sundberg."

The crowd made that murmured buzz that indicates mass surprise.

Sir Peter Melling said, "But it was that *Marvin* character. Everybody knows that."

"Everybody knows it," Blacke acknowledged, "but nobody believes it. Otherwise, Lucius wouldn't have a better arsenal than Fort Apache stacked up in his vestibule. And Marvin sure couldn't have killed Connor, the railway guard, and burned the Pullman car."

Slowly, Blacke had been wheeling himself to the middle of the dance floor, facing Jenkins and Sir Peter, who'd come to stand by him. When he got to a point about fifteen feet away, he stopped, sighed, and with an air of infinite fatigue, hitched the blanket that covered his atrophied legs higher up his body, as though protecting himself from cold.

Everything about him seemed tired. Even his voice held a slight strain. Since he was counting on talking a killer out of this crowd, that fact worried me. Feeling very self-conscious, I walked out on the floor to stand just behind him. I thought that with my new reputation as a big gunslinger in these parts, I might make someone think twice about pulling a gun. Most likely, I told myself, I was setting myself up to be perforated along with Blacke.

Tired voice or no, Blacke was still talking.

"I don't mean to say that Marvin has nothing to do with the story. Marvin was very convenient for the killer; Marvin was set up to get the blame when the killer stole the photograph of my colleague here (he hooked a thumb over his shoulder at me) with his knee on Marvin's chest. And when the posse formed, the killer tipped Marvin off; told him they were coming for him and that he'd better run, if he wanted to live.

"Let's look at things from the killer's point of view. The man—or woman, no reason to excuse the ladies yet—decides that the professor has to die. He wants to ambush the man on the way home from the party, but he also wants time to bring the professor to the railyard and ransack the Pullman. To gain time to do that, he first ambushes the vehicle immediately *behind* the professor on the trail—in this case, the one with Sundberg and Booker in it. By doing this, he's almost surely delayed discovery of the body. Not only has he stopped Booker from reaching the place he plans to dump the Professor's body before he can actually do it, he's also delayed anyone who might have been behind them, because naturally, they would stop and help.

"So the killer has time to arrange his carefully planned confusion. He waylays Vessemer, brings him to town, kills him, and drags him back to the chosen spot on the road.

"What he doesn't know is that the professor, in a rare act of presence of mind and courage, has left a clue for us to find."

There was more buzzing from the guests.

"What was this clue?" Lucius Jenkins demanded.

"Later," Blacke said. "The clue only hangs him. We only found the clue today. I want to tell you the rest, so you'll believe the clue when you see it."

"The sheriff's the person you should be telling this all to, not my guests."

"The sheriff's here, isn't he? Are you listening, Harlan?"

"I'm listening. Go ahead."

I had to look at him. Asa Harlan issuing some implied defiance to his Lord and Master. My opinion of the sheriff was struggling ever upward.

"Now, the killer might have planned the ambush when he first knows the professor is in town, or something that happened at the party might have started him off and caused the whole thing to be improvised. The question is, why take the chance? We'll get back to that later."

Blacke took his left hand from under the blanket and scratched his nose.

"But even with the killings done, the murderer isn't finished. Come Sunday afternoon, his highwayman disguise has gone over so well that no one has noticed that the photograph of Marvin, the person he plans to fix the blame on, still hasn't been discovered missing. He fixes that by knocking out the guard, Connor, and lighting a small, harmless fire on the door of the professor's Pullman car. It would be bound to be examined after that.

"The next day, after consulting with Marvin's employer, namely you, Lucius, the sheriff forms a posse to come and arrest Marvin. But

Marvin isn't there. Marvin has literally headed for the hills.

"Why did he do that? Why did he run away? Did *you* tell him who you were seeing that day, and why, Lucius?"

Jenkins was severely irritated. "Of course I didn't."

"Tell anybody?"

"I might have mentioned it at breakfast. But the house servants would have no way to get to Marvin to tell him anything."

"Didn't say they would. Now, even with Marvin dead, and his brother Frank for good measure, although Frank has nothing at all to do with the case, the killer can't help thinking. You see, I've figured all along the killer killed the professor because the professor knew him. He traveled all over the West; he came to Le Four every year at this time; he met a lot of people, and he took pictures of all sorts. Maybe he didn't recognize the character right away. Maybe the fellow had a beard or something when he'd taken his photograph in some other place. May—"

"*Yes!* Yes, that's it! He had a beard last time! He—"

I couldn't help smiling. Clayton Henry had spent most of the evening sitting near the musicians, wincing and yelling "Tempo!"

Now he had decided to help Blacke out. I cut him off.

"All right, Mr. Henry. Mr. Blacke is handling it now."

Blacke was smiling. He didn't look tired anymore, but he still held the blanket up close to him. "A witness, now. A clue and a witness."

Blacke gave his chin another left-handed scratch. "Come to think of it, why wasn't the killer worried about Mr. Clayton Henry's showing up and being as dangerous as the professor was? Was the killer the kind to simply deal with his problems as they come up, or did the professor play him for a fool again? Maybe the professor told him his assistant had quit and gone back east."

"Just a few days ago, the killer thought the clue might exist—a photographic plate left in the camera. Mr. Henry!"

"Yes, Mr. Blacke?" Henry had calmed down now. He knew where the thing was going.

"Would you join me here, and tell Mr. Jenkins about the photograph left in the camera?"

"I would be delighted." Henry told all about writing with the cigar in the semidarkness of the car, and of how we found the word "BART."

"Well, that word Bart almost defeated me. I was sure I knew who the killer was—"

Jenkins's voice was the gruffest I ever heard it. "Who, goddammit, who?"

"All right, all right, before you go shocking the ladies with your language any more than you already have.

"The killer is Sir Peter Melling."

24

"THIS IS RIDICULOUS!" Sir Peter said. "Your injuries have turned your mind, at last."

"You're out of your mind. Sir Peter is a knight, for God's sake. He's only been in the country six months. I had him checked out," Jenkins said.

"Uh-huh. Been in the country six months, most of that laid up in your guest room with a broken leg."

"Practically all of it," Sir Peter said. "I was hardly out meeting photographers and developing grudges against them."

"Then why do you ride western style?" I demanded. "In England, as in the East, where I learned to ride, we post when we ride. Your riding out with Frank the day of the gunfight was, supposedly, your first time in the saddle in this country, and you rode well enough to lead a rodeo parade. I know; you have been in the West before."

And of course, Blacke had been right. I should have seen it, I shouldn't have needed him to point it out to me. My only excuse for not noticing was that I had an appointment with a man who wanted to kill me.

"Well, of course he was in the West before," Henry said, "and he *did* have a beard. Edward took a picture of him in Newton, Kansas. He'd shot a man who'd accused him of crooked gambling."

"And there's your motive," Blacke went on. "You know, just because an Englishman has a title, we rough-cut Americans think he has money. Melling has probably been making trips here for years, cheating at cards, robbing banks, whatever he needs to, to keep the family estate going at home."

Sir Peter shook his head. "Mr. Jenkins," he said, finding the bald man squinting hard at him. He scanned the crowd for Abigail, who was standing wide-eyed beside her mother, who looked as though someone had just parted her hair with a railroad tie. "Mrs. Jenkins, I appeal to you—"

"That's just it," Blacke said. "You appealed to her. If you could marry into Lucius Jenkins's fortune, you could stay in England and live up to your title."

Melling drew himself up to his full height and sniffed, "I hold one of the oldest baronetcies in England."

"Right, right," Blacke said. "That's another thing we tend to forget. That there's differences in all you royalty and nobility and aristocracy and what all. I just knew that the English knight had done the murders, but I couldn't figure out what BART could have to do with it. Vessemer hadn't played any jokes, not about to die, and in agony from the cigar burning his fingers.

"But I was mixed up. As my colleague Mr. Booker pointed out, you're *not* a knight, you're a baronet. You're still called 'Sir,' but there's a difference. A knight has to do something brave or good to earn the title; you didn't have to do anything but be born into the right family."

"My ancestors did the earning. And if you were still a man, Mr. Lobo Blacke, I should demand satisfaction for these insults."

"Don't let that bother you. Even dead from the waist down, I'm twice the man you'll ever be. But here's the thing. Guess what the abbreviation for baronet is? Bee ay ar tee. That's what the professor was telling us, and that's what'll hang you here in the colonies."

"I think not."

Just as I had feared, Sir Peter pulled a gun from his pocket and pointed it at Lucius Jenkins.

"Come here," he said.

Jenkins stepped forward. The Englishman instantly grabbed Jenkins and kept the rich man's body on a line between himself and the sheriff, the only other armed man in the room. It was easy to see now that Sir Peter had subtly been doing that all along.

"Now, Mr. Jenkins, you and I are leaving here, and if you do exactly what I say, you may yet live to see your daughter married. Everyone get out of the way!"

The crowd drew back. He would have to go right past Henry, Blacke, and me in order to leave through the front door, and the tight smile on his face said he rather enjoyed the idea. At least, he didn't tell us to move.

Instead, he turned toward Martha Jenkins. "Good-bye, Mrs. Jenkins, and thank you for your hospitality. In parting, let me say that I find your husband a tyrant, yourself a harridan, and your precious daughter a vulgarian and a sl—"

An explosion came from under Lobo Blacke's lap robe. A spurt of red shot out from Sir Peter's forehead, and he fell heavily to the floor. Two more shots hit him while he was falling.

Women screamed. Men, too, possibly me. Still not knowing what had happened, I saw Lobo Blacke taking a brand-new black metal revolver out from under his lap robe, which had caught fire.

I knelt by him and helped him beat out the flames.

Wheelchair or not, famous gun or not, Lobo Blacke had won another gunfight.

25

THIS, IT WAS decided by mutual consent, called for an extra edition of the *Witness*. So Sunday morning found Blacke and me, assisted by Rebecca and Clayton Henry, writing and preparing the paper.

Merton Mayhew was there, too, walking on air to be in our mere *presence*. If he had been taken to Olympus to assist the gods, he could have been no more excited.

"I still don't see how all that stuff you figured out said it had to be the Englishman, Mr. Blacke."

Blacke, who in an ordinary mood would probably have told the boy to go away and figure it out for himself, was relaxed and expansive. I thought privately that it might be that he felt the adults among us might appreciate his brainpower all the better. After all, he'd been interrupted before he could explain all this last night.

"Let's look at what we knew about the killer, Merton," he said. "He had to have been at the party Saturday night, or at least near it, in order to know when Professor Ned was available to be ambushed. He had to be in town Sunday, in order to be able to set that fire. Sir Peter was; he came in with Lucius Jenkins and his family to give official statements at the sheriff's office. Miss Abigail told us that Harlan let her take a walk after she was done, and Lucius confirmed yesterday that he did the same for Sir Peter.

"But even more important than that, Merton, the killer had to be a relative stranger to the town. If he'd known that Vessemer showed up in Le Four about this time every year, he would have taken steps to protect himself long before the situation arose that would have made it possible for the photographer to see him."

"You mean, he could have faked being sick and just stayed in his room for two weeks?"

"Think he could have fooled your dad?" Blacke asked.

"Dad says, when people say they don't feel well, how can you prove they do? Besides, everything you've said so far applies equally to Mr. Booker."

Blacke was too busy laughing, so I exonerated myself. "That's true, Merton, but I came in on the train with the professor. If I'd had to kill him, I would have done it before the train ever got to town. Furthermore, I had no opportunity to tell Marvin that the posse was coming. And I was in Minneapolis when Mr. Connor was killed and the Pullman was burned."

"It was all superfluous anyway," Clayton Henry announced. "Because I recognized him from the photographs we took of the prisoners in the Newton jail. He was going by the name of English Bart."

"Bart," Rebecca said. "He must have thought himself very witty to use that name."

"I've got a few questions myself, you know, Blacke," I said.

He raised his hands, a man well contented with himself. "Ask away."

"You shot him right between the eyes."

"Well, I couldn't let him finish that sentence about Miss Abigail, could I? Besides, a man who goes into a gunfight without intending to kill his opponent is a fool."

He smiled at me sweetly.

I looked at him for a long moment.

"The next time you catch fire," I said, "I hope it's your head."

He laughed and put out a hand to shake. "If burning my head is the way to keep you around, I'll do it," he said. "You have a way of making life exciting."

"I wasn't," I informed him, "going anywhere."

Late that afternoon, the paper was made up, except for a few spaces in case anything else happened before we started printing around midnight. Merton had gone home to dinner. Henry said his leg ached and went back to his room to lie down. Rebecca had gone off, too. She was back to her schoolmarm look, but she had a warm smile for me and a look of absolute adoration for Blacke as she left.

Blacke and I were sitting around the composing room, discussing how large we should make the print run, when something did happen.

Lucius Jenkins knocked on the door and came in.

"Hello, Louis," he said.

"Hello, yourself. What brings you to town on a Sunday this time, Lucius? Not another statement for the sheriff, I hope. Heck, he was right there."

"I came to see you," he said. "You saved my daughter from a horrible situation. And you saved my life. You know he would have killed me."

"Maybe I've got my own plans for your life, Lucius. Ever think of that?"

Jenkins squinted at him but said nothing.

Blacke barked out a laugh. "Besides, if you were gone, who would I beat at checkers? Care for a game as long as you're here?"

Jenkins seemed to relax. "Sure," he said. He got ready to play once more against the man he'd betrayed, the man who meant to see him hanged. I was sure Blacke would do it someday.

But now, he just said, "Would you get the board and the men, Booker?" And I went. The game was always fun to watch.

DATE DUE			

FIC
DEA